I0737886

After the Sour Lemon Moon

After the Sour Lemon Moon

Denise Parsons

San Francisco, California

Published in San Francisco, CA

After the Sour Lemon Moon is a work of fiction. Names, characters, places, and incidents are the products of the author's imagination or are used fictitiously. Any resemblance to actual events, locales, or persons, living or dead, is entirely coincidental.

Publisher's Cataloging-in-Publication Data
Parsons, Denise Ozers.
After the sour lemon moon / Denise Parsons.
p. cm.
ISBN 978-0-615-99733-9
1. Self-actualization (Psychology)—Fiction. 2. Families—Fiction. 3. Women—Fiction. 4. California—Fiction. I. Title.
PS3616.A781 A3 2014
813.6—dc23   2014905918

Printed in the United States of America

First Edition

For those who wait

The sun rises, just like this, every single day,

yet I cannot recall the last time I took notice.

THE STATION

The train pulls slowly to a stop. I tug my suitcase down from the rack above and exit into the blue hour. It is quiet. I can hear myself breathe.

The station is small with just one all-purpose shop. Scanning shelves, I see snow globes, candy bars, and cigarettes. I turn the wobbly rack of postcards until my eyes settle on a bold CALIFORNIA written across one of the cards, a barely noticeable *Greetings from* just above. I buy it, a stamp, and a small paper cup of coffee, and sit down on one of the smooth wooden benches in the empty waiting area.

I write *I love you and miss you* on the left, and our address on the right. I lick the stamp and press it against the card. It lands slightly crooked, but is still wet, so I slide it neatly into the corner. On my way out I drop the card into the station mailbox.

WHAT IS NECESSARY

The motel is beside the station. I walk. The night is hollow, my footsteps the only sound on the street.

My room has what is necessary. I undress, step into the shower, and am surrounded by pale pink tiles. I remove the tiny beige soap from its perfectly folded paper packaging and wash my tired self. A single white towel hangs from a bar on the wall. I dry off and slip beneath the sheets of my tightly made bed.

The coffee must have been weak. I'm already tired, exhausted. I don't feel at all like myself. And then, I am asleep.

TAKING NOTICE

I wake in the dark and pull the heavy curtain aside to reveal a parking lot and a few flickering street lamps. I stare out the window until the lamps go dark and the dull glow of natural light appears in the distance. The sun is beginning its rise.

I pull the curtain further, as far as it will go, and sit down on the bed. The depth and shape of everything within the frame of the window transforms as the sun reveals itself.

The sun rises, just like this, every single day, yet I cannot recall the last time I took notice.

ONE TRUTH

But I probably shouldn't start here. I need to rewind a bit. I'm just not sure how far back I should go. Where to begin and end has always been difficult for me, and memory is a ruthless editor. She removes what she deems clutter and magnifies what most interests her. She leaves us with one truth, the only truth to which we have access.

ISIS

She stood at the cutting board and sliced an end from a heavy loaf of dark rye bread, smeared the slice with soft butter, sprinkled it with coarse salt, and placed a thick slice of sharp white cheddar cheese on top. She'd eaten the other end in exactly the same manner about fifteen minutes prior. It was the best rye bread in Chicago, at least the best on the North Side. She was partial to the ends lately, and sad this was the last, at least for the evening. The bakery had closed for the day.

Before she could take a bite she felt something funny, unlike the usual kicks. No, not yet, she thought. Not tonight.

Her daughter was supposed to be born in a room filled with sunlight, morning light. She knew she was having a girl. She knew she would be born in the morning. She was sure. It was her plan and she refused to let it happen any other way.

He was working the late shift and this was fine with her. She was in no mood for consultation. She quickly and quietly took her bread and cheese, placed it upon a napkin, rested it on her nightstand, and carefully crawled into bed.

She believed keeping very still would slow everything down. Once settled, she bit slowly through the cheese, salted butter, and into the bread—quietly, cautiously—while looking defiantly at the sour lemon moon.

It worked. I was born the next morning.

Mom named me Isis on the fifth day of May. Her choice had nothing to do with ancient Egyptian religious beliefs, she simply liked the Bob Dylan song. But before she could write Isis on my birth certificate, Dad said, 'No way.'

Mom suggested Natalie, based on her adoration of Natalie Wood.

Dad said, 'Natalie is a fat girl's name.'

They settled on Sophia, my mother's grandmother's name. Mom liked it, but Dad thought it was perfection. He'd never met my mother's grandmother, so it was not about her, or his desire to carry on a family name—he simply liked the sound of it. He looked out the window of my mom's hospital room dreamily and said, 'Sophia is the name of an interesting and beautiful woman, a woman I'd like to know. Sophia. It's perfect.'

Mom wrote *Sophia* on my birth certificate and smiled down at me. There wasn't much to me at this point. I had large dark eyes and a hint of blonde peach fuzz atop my head. That was about it.

My parents were young and hopeful. They believed in me. This is what I've been told. Mom was eighteen years old. Dad was twenty-one.

EIGHTEEN

Mom's life shifted abruptly. A high school girl one moment, a wife and mother the next.

Yes, she was only eighteen, but I wasn't an accident. She didn't give everything up for me. I was exactly what she wanted.

She told me *I* was her first love.

HAPPY

Just shy of a few years later, my sister joined us. Then we were four.

But it was really just the two of us, for a while. Mom and me. Dad worked a lot. My baby sister slept.

I'd watch Mom's soap operas and she'd watch my cartoons. She'd work through her leg-lifts and sit-ups and I'd follow along as best I could.

We were happy.

BUTTERFLY

Time passed, slowly, as it does during youth.

One warm summer night, my mother listened to the exhausted voices of her two young daughters pleading, 'One more story, Mom. Just one more. One more. Please…'

She looked down at us, dressed in our cotton nighties and tucked beneath our cool sheets, as she, tired from a day filled with two rambunctious little girls, gave in and said, 'Okay…'

'Once upon a time there was a butterfly.

The butterfly flew away.

The end.'

IMPERMANENCE

The four of us looked good together, but the bond didn't set.

TROLLOP

Eventually, Mom's friends told her she was crazy for staying with Dad. Things happened that a nine-year-old was simply too young to understand. Mom promised to tell me about those things when I was older.

She started smoking and reading *Ms.* magazine. She justified the smoking by saying she needed one thing in life that felt good. I didn't ask about the magazine.

This was the period when Mom wore her red cap sleeved t-shirt with **trollop** written across the chest. I remember the letters. They were a gummy iron-on material—bold, white, and playful.

I hated this period.

CLEAN AND NEW

My sister was seven years old. I was ten. We both had our long hair coiled into loose little buns atop our heads, soft curled wisps falling in front of our ears. We were squeaky clean, tan, and wearing new dresses—about to board an airplane for the first flight of our young lives.

We were moving to a new state and starting the school year in a new school. It was exciting, an adventure. Everything ahead of us seemed clean and new.

I must have been in denial. I wasn't thinking about leaving my home, my family. I didn't dare ask how long Mom would stay with us, or how long it would take Dad to arrive. I didn't wonder if the rest of my family had thought about what it would be like if the four of us were never together again.

But I did feel my heart sink a little as we drove away from the life we had made together. I looked out the back window of the car, through the tunnel of our tree-lined street, and watched my shrinking friends waving goodbye in the distance.

INFLUENCE

My father did not hover. There were rules, but personal space was rarely an issue for me. It was mine for the taking, perhaps too much so at times. When we moved to Arizona, Dad played the role of fun, yet strict, authoritarian. 'Do as I say, not as I do,' articulated through a grin, was one of his favorite lines. He talked a good game, but like most parents, once his children were out of sight, he rarely knew what they were up to.

I was twelve years old when I began transacting my own business. I babysat a cute little girl named Jessica. Although I quickly learned she was a four-year-old terror, I liked the independence of it all, and chose to soldier on. Her parents sold marijuana and lived in the trailer across from ours. I was always a little nervous about who might stop by when they weren't home, but I liked them. They were nice people, and they always had Doritos.

Kathy and Tommy lived beside Jessica's family. They liked to laugh and told the types of jokes children were not meant to hear. They drank a lot of wine and on occasion my father and his far-too-young girlfriend hung out with them. I've never seen my father drunk, so I'm not sure what they had in common. It must have been the jokes.

The trailer park was a place that pretty much fit the stereotype. Poorly landscaped lots, large aluminum boxes posing as homes, parents acting inappropriately, and kids hanging out by the public pool, at night, not swimming. My sister and I were strictly forbidden from hanging out, anywhere. This had always been the rule.

It is difficult to describe what Dad seemed to believe during our trailer park period. I don't think he understood we were too young to choose our own influences. He always saw the best in us and believed we were capable of great things, including immunity to our own environment. We were constantly reminded that we weren't like the rest of these, I believe his exact words were, goddamned punks. We were not to step anywhere near the flickering lights of that pool after dark, but I'd always stare curiously from the back seat of our car when we'd drive past at night. The goddamned punks seemed to be the lucky ones.

Dad tore out the shiny new manufacturer's countertops in our kitchen and installed quality butcher block. He built a well-crafted wooden fence around our lot, and landscaped Southwestern style with fine gravel and a cactus or two. He made dinner every night.

I had a crush on a boy with long dirty blonde hair that fell into waves, highlighted by the hot Arizona sun. He looked like a surfer, although there wasn't an ocean for miles. I admired him from afar. He was one of the lucky ones who hung out late by the pool. I guess his parents didn't mind. He wore faded Levi's, untucked shirts, and had beautiful green eyes. I found him dangerous, in a good way.

SECRET SELF

Arizona and I never really clicked. I blamed most of my discontent on the state.

Toward the end of high school, I began cultivating a secret self. A better version. The self I believed I was meant to be, one that would better match my name, or at least my father's beautiful perception of my name.

I filled in my gaps with novels—traveling with fictional characters to all the places I wished I'd been, meeting the people I should have met, feeling the stress of grand decisions that had not been mine to make.

It was how I eventually developed a certain air of sophistication, a surprising trait for someone of my simple background. An impressive feat, but it happened too quickly and too artificially. It left me feeling on edge with a constant fear of being found out.

CHARACTER

After college I wanted to erase my years in Arizona and return to the place I last felt normal. So I moved back to Chicago.

I had earned my undergraduate degree. My foundation was in place. It was time to outline my character, the new role I'd play.

She would be smart, but not at all pretentious. Driven, but never aggressive. Poised and sophisticated by day and slightly rebellious after hours. My model of the perfect young professional female.

Some of it was true, most of it wasn't, not yet, but it would be. I found myself quite cunning. I marched proudly into my first real job interview wearing high heels, a new suit, and glasses (non-prescription glasses). It's amazing how focused I was on branding and marketing myself before truly understanding either concept.

I was determined, but my character was only a shell. Beneath, I was far more complex, layered, murky—better. I just hadn't worked out how to exhibit those parts of myself yet.

PHOTOGRAPHY

During my first interview, the one with the non-prescription glasses, they hired me. I worked hard and moved up steadily over the course of several years, learning and becoming more of the person I pretended to be during the interview. It was a good life, but I quickly learned the corporate world was tiring and competitive.

I needed something softer in my days, something that could offer balance. So I signed up for a refresher course in photography.

Although my interest in photography began at an early age, I hadn't thought much about cameras or photographs since high school.

I began making photographs when I was about ten years old. Dad taught me how to use a light meter and to always make sure the sun was behind me when I released the shutter. I attached a red, white, and blue strap to my camera, pulled it over my head, and let it rest around the back of my neck. I wore it everywhere and took my image making very seriously, for a year or two, before other interests took over.

I returned to photography when I joined our high school yearbook staff as a photographer, but only stayed on board for a year. Not enough freedom. Too many rules.

When I called Dad and told him I'd signed up for a refresher course, he sent me the old 35mm camera, case, and my red, white, and blue strap. The man saved everything. And he'd always encouraged my interest in photography.

I bought some film and photography became my quiet escape.

I'm not sure how some are unable to locate it. The silence. I've always been able to find it. It is simply a matter of knowing what to pay attention to and what to ignore.

A camera is helpful. Focusing through a viewfinder invites concentrated attention. Noise and clutter fall away.

And then there is the subway car, or the city bus. Although both are often jammed with people, they can feel quieter than a rural library. In cities, people collapse into themselves, they create their own silence within the noise. It is easier to ignore a crowd of people than it is to ignore just a few.

I had a vision. I imagined myself gazing out a tall window from within a tiny Paris apartment—a perfectly soft cooked egg, slice of toast, and slender glass of freshly squeezed orange juice before me.

I knew the juice and toast wouldn't be a problem, but I had to work at getting my yolk to reach that soft gooey state of perfection. And I had to save some money.

So I began boiling a lot of eggs and opened a savings account.

I'd always wanted to go. I worked hard. I'd earned it. And finally, I was there, enjoying my perfect egg in the quiet of early morning.

Just as I finished, he opened his eyes—sleepy, adorable, and smiling. He was flawless.

We'd met in a cafe the night before. He'd had too much to drink. I hadn't. My instincts told me he was harmless. He slept on my sofa.

I told him I had to catch a plane. I lied. It was my first morning in Paris and I wanted it all to myself.

After he departed, I waited fifteen minutes and then dressed. I wore a cashmere sweater, jeans, and Swedish leather boots. As I gathered my things I could hear the distant chatter of the boys on the school playground below.

I descended the stairs, exited the building, and looked back up to admire my apartment. In the apartment below mine I saw an older woman in a bathrobe, curlers in her hair, looking down at me. She was shaking her head in disapproval. *No*, I thought. *There's no way*. I smiled and waved as I crossed the street. She turned away abruptly.

Oh well, I thought, looked back up at the windows to my apartment, and sighed contentedly. It was such a lovely building.

I strolled around the little island and then up and down the river for hours. Eventually I sat down at an outdoor cafe table and drank a glass of red wine for lunch. I was hungry, but the emptiness felt good, as if I was opening space for something new.

There is a self that emerges while traveling alone. The lack of companion allows one to rest in silence, ask questions, and be open to discovery.

I was somehow better in Paris. I was nicer to myself. I didn't hurry. Guilt was way down on the lowest rung. I was lonely, but it was a beautiful loneliness. I didn't mind it.

SHAKESPEARE AND CO.

It is evening. It grows later, and later, yet I hesitate. A reading. Do I really want to leave my new apartment? Paris will be my home for such a short time. It's so pleasantly warm and comforting here, and I'm feeling rather lazy. Yes, yes. I should go. No, don't make it a should. Make it a want. Okay, I want to go. I'll be happy. I know I will.

Up already. I go. It is cold, very cold, but my journey is brief.

I settle into one of the last available seats and soon she is before me, just a few feet away. It is an intimate space. A tiny Left Bank bookstore brimming with books and people. She begins. Her voice, at first curt and British, a bit rough, is soon reined in to soft. And then she finds it, she's exactly where she wants to be.

Her voice sways with perfect cadence and the chill I've brought inside with me begins to dissipate. All that was rigid is now relaxed and I begin to take in my surroundings.

Books, old and new, stacked to the ceiling—uneven columns on the verge of collapse. It is dusty and warm. The eyes around me look tired and hungry, yet patient, fully willing to wait for food and sleep. I sit quietly against the west wall of books, their spines making faint impressions in mine. The lower shelf I sit upon seems to become harder as the night progresses and I strain to keep my shifting silent.

Climbing into her world is difficult, as I am so immersed in my own. So much new. Her voice slows and then finishes.

There are questions. Why do they always seem to disappoint? And then it is over and I am jolted as all of the bodies stand at once and the wine begins to flow. But this is not my ending. I wrap myself beneath necessary layers, push through the crowd, and hurry into the icy night air beside the river.

Quiet, cold, the traffic a simple hum. Lights twinkle all around me and scattered snowflakes fall slowly as I cross the bridge and head back toward the small island.

I climb what seem a great many well worn steps and then I am sealed tightly inside, four stories up, behind my cerulean door.

HOME

My career grew, my friendships were intact, and romance in my life
rose and fell in subtle waves. I'd settled into a comfortable routine.

I was waking early to make photographs beside the river. I wanted
uninterrupted time before going into the office. It was a cool spring
morning and rather than confine myself within a bus, I decided to
walk downtown along the water, in the clean lake air.

The city was quiet, most people still in their homes showering or
brewing their first cup of coffee. The low angle of the sun with its
long shadows and soft light made everything special. I advanced
through frames of film effortlessly. None of the usual contemplation.
All I had to do was point the lens and look through the viewfinder.
There was little to disappoint.

I finished my roll of film, climbed the stairs from the river path
back up to Michigan Avenue, and walked patiently through the crowd
of harried, single focused bodies. I'd had time to acclimate. They
were much closer to sleep.

Moving back to Chicago seemed a return to where I belonged.
And my apartment, albeit small, and rather spare, was all mine. I
loved it. Revisiting photography was taking me to places inside
myself I'd forgotten existed. Everything felt right.

I'm not one to fall for the idea of fate. I believe in choice, but this
was somehow different. I started to believe it possible my life had
been mapped out all along, yet I'd been veering just slightly off
course since about the age of ten. Lately it seemed I was returning to

the original line that had been drawn for me, my body relaxing into the groove.

After work I waited for the 'L', feeling the vibration of the wooden platform as its cars passed before me. I boarded, found a seat, and swayed with the Brown Line as it slowly ambled above the street below, carrying me home.

I tossed a simple green salad and was pulling a small roast chicken with new potatoes from the oven when the phone rang. My father was being admitted to the hospital for heart surgery.

There wasn't time to think. I had to go. I left the Chicago River and the breeze off Lake Michigan to return to Arizona. The Valley of the Sun.

The Valley of the Sun, such a deceptively joyous name.

BREATHING

The only restaurant within walking distance of the hospital, the hospital with the largest cardiac wing in the metropolitan area, was McDonald's. It was a typical looking McDonald's, with one exception. It had a large and seemingly misplaced concrete fountain wedged between the dumpsters at the rear of the restaurant and the drive-thru speaker. The fountain was fully functional and trickled smugly, as if it were in the center of the Gardens of Versailles. I found it disconcerting. More than disconcerting, really. I loathed that fountain.

I repeated the cycle of spending time in the hospital, with its medicinal smell and bad lighting, eating identical hamburgers tasting of anything but beef for lunch and dinner each day, walking in the dry dead heat of Mesa, AZ, and loathing that damn fountain, until I could take no more.

I fell over the edge and existed in a steady state of nausea. I was strangely only able to stomach three things—dark rye bread, cold cucumber slices, and tinned sardines. Oh, and sour hospital coffee laden with powdered creamer and white sugar.

I'd given up my beloved cheddar cheese. It had always been a favorite food, a special treat, especially with rye bread, but all of the discussion of clogged arteries had ruined it for me.

VOLUNTEER

Dad wouldn't be able to drive for at least two months. No one raised their hand and volunteered to help him with his recovery. For Pete's sake, the man had just had his ribs sawed open. He needed me. So I took a leave of absence from work, and tried to settle into a new way of life.

I checked out of the hotel near the hospital and spent the night at Dad's, alone. He was scheduled to leave the hospital and return home the following afternoon.

That first night was overwhelming. His house was overflowing with duplicates of just about every item he owned. He had seven cameras (many in need of repair), close to thirty very similarly sized mixing bowls, and layers of unframed paintings leaning against every wall. His mounds of dirty laundry were endless and his closet was full with clean clothes. I had no idea what he'd do with his dirty clothes if he ever washed them. In his driveway, parked beside his truck, there was a beautiful burgundy Mercedes convertible. It didn't run. Trouble with the starter. The backyard held three smokers, one large and one small pizza oven, four grills, thirteen bicycles, six kayaks, and one cement mixer.

I'm not sure if he was preparing for some sort of disaster, or if he simply took comfort in compiling objects that made him feel needed. The majority of these items were not in working order and required his tinkering.

Also, he'd stopped opening his mail. He was convinced it was all bad news. Mountains of unopened mail rose from his coffee table, love seat, and dining table. His dining chairs were piled with books and long yellow notepads filled with lists and ideas.

I removed all clutter from one of the small beds in the guest bedroom, washed some bed linens, and scrubbed the guest bathroom. A small place to escape the mess. Next, I washed his bed linens and bathroom. I knew I'd barely made a dent, but there was something about unkempt beds and bathrooms I could not tolerate. I tried to ignore the rest.

SLEEP

Once Dad was home, there was the challenge of sleep. He couldn't. Not in his bed, and not in his chair. I couldn't. For fear something would happen and he'd need me.

My shins were bruised from trying to help a drugged 250-pound post-quintuple-bypass man adjust comfortably in his bed. He'd lost an integral part of the anti-snoring contraption he had come to depend upon for sleep, and I'd exhausted all means of replacing the part. He refused to try a new model.

The first night he slept I sat in the living room, limp in his La-Z-Boy chair, watched crap television, and ate an entire bag of stale generic nacho flavored tortilla chips I found in the back of a kitchen cabinet. It somehow felt like the right direction. I was too exhausted to care about my arteries. I needed something just for me, something that didn't require a fearful reading of prescription label instructions, a doctor, or demand of any sort.

That night I woke up every half hour, walked quietly into Dad's room, and listened for his breathing.

VASTNESS

Vastness. There is a need for it. At minimum, a glance from time to time. It keeps that little pilot light inside of us going. We need to look out into the unknown, where the distance blurs.

I still feel Lake Michigan calling me. There is something very specific about this particular lake, as seen from Chicago. For me, the imprint was set in place early. Although I was far too young to remember, I've heard many stories of my early days beside this lake. I began visiting its edge when I was a mere infant.

The story my father retells most involves a two-year-old me, carefully placed in a little bike seat mounted on the front of his street bike. We would ride along the lake together, Dad pedaling, while I quietly gazed at the sites. He tells me how easy it was to be with me in those days. I was very agreeable at the age of two. Never an argument, no complaints, and I always let him select my riding outfits. He was twenty-three years old.

And before I was born, my parents spent their childhoods and teen years beside this lake. Looking out from the lakefront in Chicago resembles what most people imagine when they think of looking out onto the ocean. There is no other side, not visible. This is the vastness I crave.

When I visit Chicago the first thing I want to see is the lakefront, and there is an anxiousness until I find my way there. When I see it, my heart and breathing slow, and I believe there are answers to my questions. I haven't asked my father what he found most appealing about those rides along the lakefront, but I have a feeling he too was seeking answers.

It is embedded in me, this desire for vastness, and its fulfillment. I can tap into aspects of it with ocean coastlines, sometimes rivers, or other lakes; even a pond can offer something, on occasion, if I'm desperate enough.

The Valley of the Sun is an affectionate name for a shallow pit. It is strangled by mountains serving as tall walls the interior inhabitants cannot see beyond. But when there are clouds the sky feels big. It has depth. It is vast. It is one of the most beautiful skies I've ever seen. The clouds cannot be called upon, they come when they choose to come. Albeit seldom, they do arrive. Year after year. One must remember to look up often, or risk missing the fleeting glimpse of vastness, and suffer the long wait for its return.

CAREFREE

I drove Dad's truck about an hour north and just slightly west, to Carefree, AZ. I parked, jumped down from the truck, pulled the hem of my dress up, knotted it about mid-thigh, and stepped into our creek. Well, it was no longer ours, but we had once owned that particular portion of the creek, and the ten acres of desert surrounding it. It was still as quiet as I remembered. The gentle pressure of the current against my legs brought back memories of a much younger version of myself, wading around in the same creek with my little sister, a cool respite from the dry heat of the Sonoran Desert.

Dad had left his former self in Chicago and decided to create someone new and improved. We were along for the ride. He loved us, but the move was for him. They had schools in Arizona. We'd be fine. He grew his short curly hair long and stopped shaving until he became a very tan and handsome Grizzly Adams look-alike.

He bought the Carefree land with the help of a local real estate agent. I believe her name was Joan. She had long tan legs and wore pastel suits with matching high heels. Joan showed my sister and me how a sundial worked and bought us soft serve ice cream cones at Dairy Queen. Back then, when my sister and I were just little girls, not much else existed out there. There was Joan, the Dairy Queen, and a dark little pub that served a fantastic fish sandwich. The Horny Toad. The Horny Toad had no problem with eight and eleven-year-old girls sidling up to the bar and ordering sandwiches. While we ate, a few stools down, Dad and Joan would talk about Dad's potential land purchases.

It did not occur to me back then that Dad's relationship with Joan might have reached beyond real estate, which is surprising, I usually knew. I had him figured out at a very early age. Perhaps I was distracted by the novelty of the new-to-me desert landscape. I now wonder if she was one of Dad's many women. Joan did spend a lot of time with us, and Dad did not waste his time charming women whose bedrooms he would not be visiting. Sure, there was the usual wink and flirtation with any female who crossed his path—grocery store cashiers, our teachers, the mothers of our friends—but these were only small commitments, with easy escapes.

Carefree hadn't changed much since the Joan period. There was a new bar, where motorcycle types congregated, beside The Horny Toad. There were more well-groomed adobe style houses trying to blend in with the desert. But the area remained calm and still.

From my place in the creek, all I saw was wild; nothing residential or commercial in sight. It appeared electricity and running water still had not found their way onto the property, unless you counted the creek. I wondered how our lives would be different if Dad built our home in Carefree, and not sold the land. I wondered what had happened to Joan. I couldn't imagine her old. For me, Joan will live forever in her late twenties.

Dad found more land at the base of the Superstition Mountains, at the edge of the Tonto National Forest. The view was amazing and the property had access to water and electricity. It is where he built our house. My best friends lived in trailers on stretches of desert, in rickety houses beside horse corrals, and one lived in a little pink house in town.

This place beside the Superstition Mountains is where I met a boy named Joe. At the time, it was a special relationship filled with all-important adolescent discovery. But in retrospect, it was only a fleeting moment in my history. I wanted more and I moved on.

My moving on became a pattern. It always worked out for the best. Onward and upward! Until I regressed. When you're weak you can't look forward, you can only rest in the past.

QUIET-RITER

As soon as Dad was able to walk and begin rehabilitation he wanted to visit the Salvation Army store to shop. And he wanted to shop every single day. I was his driver.

Attempting to dissuade him from adding to his immense collection of belongings was futile, so I decided to go with the flow. Almost. I convinced him daily shopping was just too much and we became weekly regulars at the Salvation Army store. He spent little money, yet he never left without a purchase of some sort.

During one of our weekly shopping visits I noticed a petite Quiet-Riter typewriter in a compact leather carrying case. It was half-price day and Dad insisted on buying it for me. Of course, it needed work, something to do with the tension of the ink ribbon hugging its spool. Surprisingly, he did not set the typewriter project aside. He fixed it for me, the same day we brought it home. I'm not sure what came over him. He must have known I was reaching maximum capacity with my tolerance for his company.

I was happy to have the typewriter. I'd always preferred the written word. Unlike conversation, it allowed for review, and proper editing. My tendency to get directly to the point was my problem. It made people uncomfortable.

I grew accustomed to beginning letters closer to the middle of the first page, knowing I'd have to backtrack and fill in the open space at the top with forced pleasantries and polite interest in the recipient's life. The process felt unnatural, but I bent to comfort others.

It wasn't a lack of interest in other people. I was interested. I'd always been interested. I simply favored a slower structure, one that allowed me time to think before easing into an interaction. Face-to-face contact opened the door too quickly and often led to misspoken words and regret.

While Dad napped, I found some blank paper, placed it behind the roller, and turned the knob. Then I just sat there, at a small clearing I'd made in the mess on the dining room table, and looked at the clean white page. I almost wanted to leave it that way. It had so much possibility. My hands moved to the keys and I began, from memory, to type a poem I'd written in high school. I recalled each and every word, each break, and the boy for whom the poem was written—Joe.

WHITE BIKINI

I know I was locked out of the house. I do not recall how this happened, why I was without my key, or why my sister wasn't with me. It was long ago and some fragments of detail have broken free from this memory. I do know that I was sixteen. Also, very important at the time, I owned a white bikini. I loved that white bikini.

We lived on a patch of Arizona desert just beneath the middle of the state, at the base of the Superstition Mountains—the land I mentioned earlier. The Lost Dutchman's Gold Mine was rumored to be buried up in those mountains, somewhere. The story of the Lost Dutchman was usually referenced in a comical sort of way, but I wasn't quick to dismiss such things. I was unsure, but kept an open mind.

After living most of my life in Chicago, this was Wild West territory. Dad grew a beard, shot rattlesnakes, and decided to build his own house. When we were home alone, I was instructed by Dad to *shoot to kill* anyone daring to set foot on our property and come near my sister and me. I would always nod in agreement, but secretly decided if such a situation occurred I'd go for the intruder's knees.

My English teacher was discussing poetry and she had my ear. We were experimenting with various forms and she responded to my work in a way that made me feel I had promise. I really needed that at the time. I think she knew. I'll never forget her. Mrs. Kasper.

I was a difficult student to engage. Fickle would be a generous description. But this felt different. It was as if the subject had been created for me. It didn't feel like work at all.

I daydreamed about words, placing them side by side, moving them from line to line, pronouncing them out loud, slowly, feeling every syllable, and then shaping and reshaping it all, over and over again.

So when I realized I was locked out of the house, it wasn't such a big deal. The school bus had gone and even the dusty cloud it left behind was mostly settled. There wasn't much I could do. I decided to begin a new poem, in my head, hoping I'd be able to memorize it and write it down later.

It wasn't for class, it was for him. Joe. I was attempting to articulate my feelings. They say love at such a young age is not real love, but I disagree. Honestly, the core of what I believe to be love now and what I believed back then, they aren't so different.

I fidgeted and shifted about on a large boulder until I felt comfortable, and then I began. I wrote and wrote, without paper or pen, and the time passed without my notice. I had not seen or heard a single thing for hours when Dad's truck broke through the quiet, kicking up gravel on our lonely road.

I looked up to a sinking sun, every dirty shrub and cactus glowing, and felt the air beginning to cool. I'd written a poem.

I don't know what happened to my white bikini, but the poem, it stayed with me.

TIME TRAVEL

Driving the old pickup truck and arguing with Dad over endless trivialities took me directly back to my teen years, and like a teenager with close to two more unwanted months in The Valley of the Sun ahead of her, I reacted impulsively.

I longed for things to be that simple again, to be as naive as a teenager. I wondered if Joe lived nearby, if he'd returned to his hometown, or if he was somewhere far away, hoping to leave it all behind.

I imagined his mother living in the same house they lived in while we were in high school. I couldn't see her anywhere but there for the rest of her life. She was a woman of routine, a woman who did not welcome change. I remembered how comforting her routines felt to me back then. Her set meal times. The way she'd shower before bed each night.

Unlike his mother, Joe had always fought routine. Finding him anywhere in the vicinity was a long shot, but I had nothing to lose, or so I thought. I reached into the closet and pulled down the phone book.

I opened the fat book, flipped the thin pages to find the letters of his last name, and moved my finger down the page. His mother's name was there. Right below it was his.

AGAIN

I wanted to see him. I needed something and hoped he might be it. My vision of him was of the boy I knew in high school, the one who'd made me laugh. I was desperate for laughter.

When we finally met, I did not recognize him. He walked right up to me and still had to introduce himself. He'd changed to such an extent I didn't even know it was him. He looked so old. That's all I could think. So old. And it wasn't his skin or his hair, it was the heavy look in his eyes. He told me I looked just the same and was even kinder to me than he'd been the first time around.

He told me he'd met her in Guam. There was an accidental pregnancy and they'd married quickly. The relationship barely had time to begin before it was over. She stayed in Guam with their son. She was remarried now and her new husband had adopted his son. Joe had agreed to stay out of their lives. I didn't know how much of his sadness was based on this decision and how much he'd carried with him from his youth. Seeing him reminded me of this burden he'd lugged around back then, the heaviness that weighed him down. This vulnerability, it had been a large part of what initially attracted me to him.

I rested in his kindness and the good memories of my youth. We were both sad, and being sad together always feels better than being sad alone. Yes, it stunts healing, but I wasn't open to rational thought at the time.

Everything that didn't make sense about us when we were teenagers made even less sense all those years later. The differences that polarized us had multiplied. We ignored it all.

POEMS

Thoughts of writing more poetry danced in my mind, romantic thoughts of it just flowing from me, perfectly, no need for editing. But it didn't play out quite that way.

Reading was inspiring. I used my dad's library card and kept a book of poems beside my bed at all times.

I recall opening one of those books, a Grace Paley collection, to the first poem, and stopping at the beginning of the fourth stanza:

a person should be in love most of
the time

And I stopped. *Yes,* I thought.

A house that is filled with clutter does not make one feel less empty. I somehow sat in the chaos of that house and attempted to write new poems. I needed to write. I craved it.

I typed my work on the Quiet-Riter. I liked the quirky imperfections of the keystrokes. I pulled draft after draft from the roller and took a pen to each. There were circles, arrows, lines drawn through words, and messy notes in the margins. Some poems I would finish in a day and some, to this day, remain buried in Dad's house somewhere, unfinished.

The poems weren't very good, but it didn't matter.

SPARE KEY

I saw what I wanted to see and ignored what I didn't.

Joe surprised me during his lunch hour and showed up with a quiet knock at Dad's front door. Dad was napping. He didn't hear a thing.

We drove over to Joe's mother's house. She was attending her book club meeting. We took her spare key from beneath the potted rubber tree plant in the courtyard and opened the front door.

It all looked the same. The furniture, the paintings and photographs on the walls, even the light.

I sat down at the kitchen table and watched while Joe removed an array of bottles, jars, bags, and packages from the refrigerator.

When we were in high school he'd made the most fantastic sandwiches. There weren't any special ingredients, they were all rather pedestrian, but he worked magic with them. It reminded me of my mother's salads and her perfectly buttered toast. Seemingly simple things I could not replicate. Methods that could not be taught.

I watched as he moved through every step of the process with loving care. Nothing was hurried. Each cucumber and tomato slice was thin and precise. Meat and cheese were distributed evenly atop the first slice of bread, then tomato, cucumber, and salt and pepper. The perfect amount of mayonnaise was slathered onto the second slice before he placed it gently on top. He cut the sandwich into two neat triangles and placed each one on a plate beside a handful of salted potato chips. Then he poured two glasses of cold milk.

His mom still maintained her well-stocked kitchen. Everything in order. She did not miss a beat. She didn't even eat sandwiches. This was all for him, his brother, and his sister, should they choose to stop by. *Amazing*, I thought.

Joe didn't think it was amazing. It was what he grew up seeing. His mother was the foundation everyone stepped upon to get where they needed to be.

I whispered a thank you to his mom.

This entitlement reminded me of my childhood. I remembered seeing my mother and my aunts during family gatherings. All of their preparation in the beginning. All of their tidying at the end. It was what was expected of them and I did not see them question it. I hung out with my dad and my uncles. The women seemed to have a rotten deal. I decided way back then I'd never get married.

The sandwich? It tasted like youth.

It all moved so quickly. A call, a first date, a sandwich. And then, the girls.

I couldn't refuse them. Our foundation was far from solid, but this did not seem a strong enough reason to say no.

They arrived a perfect set. And then we were four.

WINTER

We were in the midst of a romantic getaway. *Romantic getaway*, even the sound of it was desperate. Joe's mother watched the girls while we stayed in a familiar cozy cabin filled with soft blankets, a wood stove, and an incredibly comfortable bed.

The first morning was sunny and warm, for winter. Sunlight heated the foot of the bed. I looked outside. It was beautiful. A perfect day for a hike or picnic. Instead I drove into town, alone, with an excuse of buying pastries for our breakfast. I bought the pastries and then wandered aimlessly along Main Street, unable to appreciate what was before me, yet not at all interested in returning to the cabin.

When I did return, Joe pretended to be engrossed in yesterday's newspaper. I paged through an old magazine I'd found on the coffee table. We used to come up here to escape, I thought. Just the two of us. We didn't want any clutter, any distractions. Now we search for both.

And it was just the beginning. We had six more days of *romance* ahead of us.

Suddenly, he stood up and said he was leaving the cabin to visit the main house on the property to give his brother a quick call. For what, I had no idea, nor did I care.

An hour and a half later he returned, after chatting with his brother, a coworker, and having a long lovely conversation with his mother. He walked in the door and I looked at him in disbelief.

'A quick call?' I demanded. He shrugged and went back to the newspaper.

Was I the one with the problem? Should I have understood his need to get away? Maybe. Maybe I was just jealous. I was starting to question everything about myself.

We'd collapsed into a wilted mess, again. I was reliving high school, way too late in my life, and it wasn't as fun as one might imagine. My reasons had lost their way and my motivation for locating them had dwindled to none.

A FUNERAL

A phone call. There was to be a funeral. A family friend I hadn't seen since childhood. Someone Joe and the girls had not met. It was in Wisconsin. No need to pack up the entire family. I'd go alone.

I booked a rental car and plane ticket, packed an overnight bag, put on a black dress, and headed toward the airport, sure there would be a room available in the quiet, small town motel I remembered.

I arrived late. It was dark, but I could see how little had changed. The motel did have an available room. I ate the banana in my tote bag for dinner, undressed, pulled a clean white t-shirt over my head, and fell asleep watching the news.

I was still in bed when a harsh ray of summer sunlight shot through the space between the dark curtains and hit me right between the eyes. Still tired, I showered with the small complimentary soap, dried myself with a thin white towel that smelled of bleach, and dressed in yesterday's clothes.

I stopped at the local mini-mart for breakfast. A peanut donut and small coffee. I took a bite and sip and headed toward the on-ramp.

I knew I couldn't tell a soul what I was thinking. The truth was I wasn't at all surprised things had turned out this way. The news hadn't really shocked me. It seemed to make sense. My reaction had been a strange feeling, sort of numb, or blank. I thanked God for my dark sunglasses. I hadn't cried. I didn't even feel sad.

I hadn't thought about him in so long, but as they began lowering the casket into the grave, it all started coming back to me. That one summer. I was eight or nine years old and he was about a year or so older. So long ago, but still, I'd never forgotten.

RUNT

I sat up in bed and scanned the camper. Everyone was still, eyes closed. Nothing but the hum of slow steady breathing. 'Perfect!' I whispered to myself and pulled my cotton nightgown up over my head, tossed it onto my pillow, stepped into my jean shorts, and pulled on a t-shirt. Swiftly. Silently. As if it were all one graceful move. Before departing, I took the hidden plastic sandwich bag from beneath my pillow and slipped it into my back pocket. Stepping as lightly as possible, I made my way toward the door, opening it just enough to slide out, and closing it gently behind me. I wiped the dew from the outside doorknob onto the front of my shorts and jumped off the tiny camper patio into the sand.

The birds were still asleep, but the fish weren't. I breezed past the array of tents, coolers, lawn chairs, and sandals as I made my way toward the pier. The shaded sand was cool on my bare feet.

The wood planks of the pier were warm from the morning sun. They felt good. My pace slowed as I walked purposefully over the wood, feeling each warm knot and each thin cool open space between planks.

I settled down at the end of the pier, seated as if poised on a throne, my spine perfectly straight. My bare feet dangled over the edge as I looked out across the lake. This early, it was all mine. I owned it. I removed the slice of bologna from the sandwich bag and shoved the empty bag back into my pocket. The lake was calm and the sandy bottom visible through the pale green water.

I tossed a pinky nail size piece of bologna into the water and watched. A beautiful streak of blue and gold shot up from deeper water and devoured it. A bluegill. I recognized some fish from fishing with Dad and my uncles, but

I knew this one because it was the state fish of Illinois, my state. The bluegill tracked back in search of more. I dropped another bit and watched the same fish dart toward it. He was so quick. He seemed to be inhaling the bologna. Curious, I tossed the remainder of the big round slice into the water, wondering how the fish would handle such a thing. The larger slice floated on the surface of the water. The bluegill pecked at it briefly, like a hen, and then gave up. I felt bad and decided to revert back to bite-size offerings tomorrow. The bologna drifted away from the pier and out into the lake, and the bluegill disappeared. It was obvious that he was not entertained. I was sure he looked up at me and frowned before moving on with his day.

I heard the echo of a motorboat engine being tugged on the other side of the lake, the satisfied hum of the motor, and then footsteps on the pier. I sighed unhappily while turning around. 'Oh, great,' I whispered beneath my breath. The last time I'd seen him he'd pontificated on the joy of pinching his baby brother each time he'd fall asleep, causing him to wake crying. He'd taken great pride in getting away with it without his mother ever figuring out he was the cause.

If I'd been wearing my bathing suit I would have jumped into the lake and swam the way of the bluegill. But here, fully clothed, and at the end of the pier, I was cornered—forced to socialize with the runt. I didn't know exactly what runt meant, but I remembered it being used in Charlotte's Web to describe the small pig no one wanted, and the little /nt/ sound at the end of the word felt appropriately curt and condescending.

Most disturbing was the story his brother had told me. Last summer the runt had buried a live toad and turtle and let them die beneath deep mounds of sand. I imagined them gasping for air and inhaling the dry granules. It was horrifying. What type of person was capable of such things? He was a bad seed. I thought of this incident each time I saw him and always looked at him with disdain. He seemed to enjoy it.

He'd come to inform me my father was looking for me. He wanted to discuss the stash of bottles I'd been collecting at the campground dump. How could anyone have found those? I thought. They were hidden. He grinned like the Cheshire Cat. 'Runt,' I mumbled as I stomped away, up the pier, and back toward the camper to face Dad.

I'd been warned about wandering around the dump, and especially about collecting items there, but I loved it. It wasn't a typical dump; well, not what I imagined a typical dump to resemble. I hadn't actually seen another dump, but this one was like visiting a toy store where everything was free. Why was I banned from such a place? I'd been collecting empty soda bottles for Mom. The bottles would serve as vases. I'd fill them all with wildflowers and place them around our campsite to surprise her. It would be like a wedding, but better because Mom's happiness would be the only reason for celebration, nothing more.

Midway to our campsite I decided to turn around and head up to the outdoor church. I thought Dad might cool down if I gave him a little time. The church was empty. I had not been to a service, but I loved visiting the quiet space when it was vacated. I sat down on the concrete theater-like steps and looked at the stage.

I could pray, I thought. No, if any of that stuff actually works, I should save it for something big, something really important.

RETURN

After the funeral and a quick stop at a deli in town, I pulled up to a giant log in the old campground parking lot and turned off the ignition.

I walked toward the pier with a brown bag in my right hand. It contained a package of bologna, a salami sandwich, and an Orange Crush.

My black dress and high heels were glaringly out of place, but I didn't think of it, not even for a minute.

I sat down at the edge of the pier and opened the package of bologna. I tore away a small piece and dropped it into the water. A soft series of circles rippled out around it. I bit into my salami sandwich and watched the bologna rest on the surface of the water as I sipped my Orange Crush. No bluegill. Nothing but quiet.

My beautiful black shoes dropped from my feet into the lake. I watched them float away, beside the bologna.

THE DAY AFTER

The next day, unplanned, I bought a pair of black shoes, and drove into Chicago. Straight into the belly of the beast. I hadn't returned in years. The city remained strong, loud, and sturdy.

After checking into a hotel I decided to walk toward the lake. I'd only walked a block or so before I stopped.

There it was, towering above me, at the corner of Washington and Dearborn. The fabulous Picasso sculpture I worshipped as a child. It always looked like a giant lion to me. How had so much time passed since that little girl discovered this commanding piece of art? My eyes grew wet. I exhaled and walked on.

The Buckingham Fountain was next. Just as magnificent as I remembered. Everything felt so solid, so permanent.

And then, the lake. Vast as ever.

ANOTHER DAY

I had this haunting feeling I'd never return, so I extended my stay. Just one additional day. I needed more time.

I wanted to feel the familiar vibration of the elevated wood plank platform at State and Lake, and the rumble of the Brown Line heading north toward the Fullerton stop. The stop still existed, but I realized it was one of only a few things in my old neighborhood that had remained. Favorite shops had closed. My old apartment building had been partially renovated and left sadly unoccupied. The nearby children's hospital was shuttered.

What remained reflected the sadness of returning to a familiar place after having spent time away. There was the photographer who had lost the hop in his step, and his studio. The man behind the office window, seated at the same poorly lit desk, the same sad look in his eyes. All optimistic fantasies of them evolving or moving on to something new were taken away by the bold face of reality.

The shopkeeper's hair had gone gray and brittle. She'd turned that corner—the one round which she'd begun to vanish—where the demons take charge. The stage where even those who adored her only spoke of how beautiful she once was. The lost elasticity of youth. I could see her former self hidden beneath, but also noticed she'd become invisible to those young or new. They had not known her earlier. Her smile meant nothing to them. All they saw was an old woman.

I wondered when it happened, and feared the day those demons would begin grasping at my heels.

Clark Street was as grimy as ever, perhaps even more so. It was comforting.

SOMEONE ELSE'S LIFE

And then it became clear. The reason I so often asked myself, *Who am I?*

I'd been living someone else's life, and not just Joe's; before his it was another's, and before his there was someone else. I wasn't sure when I'd last fully inhabited my own life.

Sure, I carved out private little spaces for myself. In fact, I'd become a master at doing so. But those spaces were always carved into someone else's world. It was time to build my own.

THESE PEOPLE

Another dinner party. *Who are these people?* It was all I could think as I stared out the window.

It was as if I'd been sleepwalking for years. These people were not mine, not one of them. And I didn't know who my people were. If I somehow found them, would they understand me, see me as one of their own?

I'd clearly let things rest in the wrong state for too long. I needed to find my people soon, or go it alone.

INADEQUACY

I missed the beautiful feeling of inadequacy. Some may find it a strange feeling to long for, but it's really not. Inadequacy reminds us of the innocence and discovery abundant in youth.

I'd last felt it when visiting a young man with whom I'd become romantically involved while living in Chicago. We had traveled to his hometown, Santa Barbara, CA. It was an evening we met up with one of his college friends for cocktails at sunset.

They passionately discussed South American politics. I nodded and laughed every so often, knowingly, while in truth I had no idea who or what they were discussing. I didn't feel obligated to understand. I just let it all wash over me, like a challenging poem.

They were both younger than me. How did they know such things? It seemed inherent. I didn't mind. I liked them knowing what I didn't. It made the world feel larger. I had time. I'd learn. I'd find a way.

Time passed. I changed. I was different in many ways, but I hadn't stopped enjoying that feeling. Not knowing inspired me.

I'd somehow found myself in a know-it-all role I did not want or feel I'd earned. The bright-eyed hopeful requests for me to dig into my well of information were terribly uncomfortable. I wanted to reach. I missed being around people who helped me grow. I hoped the girls were still too young to be affected, but I knew better.

AT THIRTY-TWO

At thirty-two I still looked quite good, especially in a ponytail. Definitely not my age. Bartenders and grocery clerks continued to card me. I had recently started to wonder how long it would go on, but had to admit its ending did frighten me.

It was August and so hot. I'd walked in from the grocery store, removed my clothes, filled the bathtub with cold water and two trays of ice cubes, and stepped in.

I leaned back into the cool water. What the hell was I doing? How had I landed back in the desert? Actually, the landing made sense. It was the staying that was far more difficult to defend.

I needed to clean the house and get the food ready before people started arriving for the game. Instead, I soaked in cold water and stared at the ceiling.

'I don't want to die here,' I said aloud. 'And I hate football.'

Before anyone got home, I got out of the tub, pulled my hair up into a ponytail, grabbed my purse, tossed in one pair of panties and my contact lens solution, and walked out the door. I drove north until I saw pine trees, rolled down all of the car windows, and took a deep breath.

I bought a jar of peanut butter and checked into the next motel I saw. Above the large, empty parking lot the letters on the marquee read:

To Those Who Appreciate Wisteria and Sunshine
VACANCY

My room was clean. The lady at the front desk was friendly. I sat on a chair out by the little concrete pool, ate peanut butter with a plastic spoon, and watched the sun set. I didn't see any wisteria, but I enjoyed the quiet. I think I was the only customer in the motel.

It felt so good.

SURVIVORS

My family. We are far from perfect, but we are a species of survivors. Both my father's side, and my mother's.

We can endure more than we know. I've seen it in action, on more than a few occasions. This does not mean I wanted to test myself, but I thought it good to remember, just in case.

MOTHERHOOD

Some open themselves to soul searching, hoping it will lead to discovery. And then to happiness.

For mothers, there is the guilt of happiness, happiness unrelated to their children. What if a mother searches and finds happiness elsewhere, outside of her family? What if her happiness is attached to behavior unbefitting a mother?

It is widely believed that if a mother leaves her family there is something irreparably wrong with her, something rooted in her core being, something present long before she was a mother.

The men who leave are charming, wild, not the type to settle down. They are always forgiven with a smile and a shrug. Poor guy, he couldn't help himself.

DON'T STAY

My tiny white lies grew into monsters. I read the same poems, over and over, unable to find meaning.

The Valley of the Sun was a place where much of it felt like no place at all. Perhaps there was something of value buried beneath the surface, but what I saw was stripped of all character. It left me thirsty and hungry, for so many things—unable to fill the empty spaces.

The young became old without wisdom. The dry air and hot sun were for the palo verde and the prickly pear, not the miles of black asphalt or the lawns made of pebbles painted green.

The land of sand colored houses and parched skin. I never fit in, yet it became part of me.

Joe was comfortable. For him it was home. He was born, raised, and returned to it.

My girls were still young. They could be swept away, transplanted elsewhere. I hoped I hadn't made it their home, the place to which they'd always return.

ADAPTATION

Affinity to adapt. This was my problem. Settling into the wrong types of relationships and then insisting I make them work. I excelled in this area, but my success was never sustainable.

It always began with so much optimism, but inevitably I'd come to my senses and realize my need to move on. I wouldn't want to give up, but eventually I'd realize failure was inevitable, and I'd be gone.

I so wanted to be in a successful relationship. I thought I could will it into existence. I wanted to believe it was possible, but I was like a strange plant that required special care—only able to truly thrive in a very specific climate, next to a certain house, beside a eucalyptus tree.

JOY

The house was empty. I'd straightened, washed the morning dishes, and was about to move on to the laundry. On my way to the washing machine I heard the postman open and shut our mailbox, so I dropped my armful of laundry onto the sofa and headed out the front door.

It was awful out there, like breathing in an oven. I'd tried to grow used to it, again. But I hadn't grown numb. Not yet. I still swallowed the heat. My skin felt thin, depleted of the moisture it once absorbed while living in a humid city beside a lake.

I pulled bills and grocery circulars from the mailbox, and then a postcard. I turned it over to look at the postmark. It was from Chicago. One of my former photography instructors had drawn black lines through her name and address and added mine, along with a new stamp and a quick note:

I immediately thought of you.
x,
Joy

I'd sent her a note updating my address when I moved. I couldn't believe she kept it.

Joy was inspiring. She taught photography and I don't know what else, but I imagined her life rich and full. I loved seeing the world through her eyes. She lectured in her socks and typically wore a clean, but wrinkled oxford type shirt, one sleeve pushed up to her elbow while the other inevitably fell to her wrist. Her hair was a lovely mess of salt and pepper, haphazardly pulled up, with soft curls outlining her face. She was beautiful because she had other things on her mind. Bigger, better things. She saw potential in me I did not see in myself.

The postcard briefly outlined some sort of artists' residency program in Northern California, a place called West Marin. A one-year program. Artists working in all media were encouraged to apply.

I was clearly committed elsewhere, but I decided to submit my work anyway. I cannot really explain why. Perhaps it was simply craving the fuel of someone believing in me. So I began digging through my old work, boxes of negatives and prints of the lake, the river, the still life images I used to stumble upon in my old apartment. They were all so far from who I had become. I feared I was better then, but wanted the work I submitted to represent my true and current self. I wanted to show them who I was at that precise moment in time, to see if I had anything left.

I pulled my dated film from the freezer, loaded my camera, and kept it close. I decided to listen to what spoke to me when I was alone. Nothing premeditated, and no conceptual crap. They wanted to see ten to twenty 8x10 prints from photography applicants. No statement, titles, or explanations of work were to be included. Just a name and return address.

LIKE BEING BORN

I remember reading something Annie Dillard wrote. I'd jotted it down on a piece of scrap paper and used it as a bookmark:

Opening up a summer cottage is like being born in this way: at the moment you enter, you have all the time you are ever going to have.

The longer I waited, the longer I delayed my beginning, which I knew would shorten my middle, and expedite my end.

THE OTHER SIDE

There was wind and rain in the valley. The usual stagnant air was whipping, although still trapped within the valley walls. I was near surrender, having grown tired from jumping up and trying to see what was on the other side.

I knew I was angry, but I don't think I knew I'd stopped believing in myself. I'd become one dimensional, there to serve. I hadn't stopped to consider how little an empty soul had to offer.

Then the postcard arrived and reminded me what it felt like to be praised, that shiny feeling of recognition. I wanted more.

ACCIDENTAL HABITS

We use such a small percentage of our surroundings. What can appear so grand upon arriving in a new place gets whittled down with time until large segments are eliminated from our field of vision.

Much can be avoided, without even knowing one is doing so. Shops, entire buildings, houses, and restaurants vanish. We no longer see these structures as we walk along the streets.

We embrace what we choose to prioritize, or we fall into accidental habits. Without even acknowledging our shifts in behavior, we carve a unique groove into a place. We make it our own.

The place becomes something altogether different as the groove deepens; sometimes so different it deserves a new name. But creating a new name isn't part of the way things work in our world. We share the same name for the same place, yet we all view it differently.

Each individual groove becomes an individual place. It's all we see. The square mile that holds the structure I call home at its center is seen differently by every person who passes through its perimeter.

Does this happen with people, too? Like place, can neglected pieces of the self disappear?

TEN NEGATIVES

I knew which exposures were best before I even developed the film. A look at the contact sheet confirmed my decision. I wasted no time making my final prints—all straight, raw, no manipulation. It went quickly and was so clear. Although the deadline for submissions was three months away, I dropped my prints into the corner mailbox a week after receiving Joy's postcard.

POETRY NOTES

While rummaging through photography boxes in the garage, I found an old leather bound book of poetry, *A Treasury of the World's Best Loved Poems.* It belonged to my mother.

Her maiden name was written on one of the blank pages in the front of the book. Notes were penciled in the margins. The remnants of a pressed rose from my father, before he was my father, was set between pages near the center of the book.

I liked reading what she noticed, yet she seemed a different person. Not the woman I'd come to know as my mother—someone else.

VITAL

I was tired of holding up the foundation, being so vital. I wanted to shed my importance and become a mere cog, a simple expendable part of the whole. Insignificant. Just for a year. If I could promise myself one year of focusing only on myself I knew I could recover all I'd lost and wanted returned.

ACCEPTED

My application was accepted and I wasn't shocked. It was not that I saw myself as incredibly talented, it was just what I saw happening next.

TANGLES

I sat at the kitchen table. On autopilot, I combed tangles from my long wet hair. There was still an hour before anyone else would wake. I'd traded in my dislike of waking up early for an hour of silence and coffee while my hair dried.

I was thinking of the book I finished reading yesterday. I'd already forgotten how it ended. Odd. After some thought I realized I almost always forgot how books ended. Perhaps it was my not wanting them to end. I recalled the general atmosphere of each book I'd read and could easily return to that feeling. But the endings, they fell away.

Endings. I never liked them. For better or worse, each one left me deflated.

STILTS

We were to arrive one week prior to the official start date of the residency. The goals being to begin our part-time jobs, move into our new homes, and start to settle into the community.

This idea worked perfectly for me. I adjust slowly to change and need time to acclimate to a new environment.

No one in the valley knew of my departure and no one in Northern California knew a moment of my past, beyond ten 8x10 photographs.

I pulled it off. I would have a full year to smooth my feathers, make sense of my life, decide how to move forward.

I had something specific in mind. I wanted to put my life up on stilts and rebuild my foundation. I'd seen it done before, with a house. It was possible, I thought, with a life, too.

I hid my packing list beneath our mattress. It was incredibly spare, I wrote it more for inspiration than practicality. There were few items listed—an extra pair of jeans, white t-shirts, bras, panties, socks, sandals, a jacket, and my light blue scarf. I always carried a toothbrush and small tube of paste with me, so I'd have those, and what I was wearing, including my loaded camera and strap. I tucked a family photograph and an old postcard into the outside pocket of my suitcase so I wouldn't forget them later. I'd buy anything else I needed. I was ready.

I'd depart on my birthday, a necessary gift to myself. They'd understand, eventually.

ESTABLISHING RESIDENCY

Each artist was expected to give back to the community as part of a work-study program. There would be part-time work in the library, a bakery, a small tile business, assisting a local painter, the permaculture institute, and the local newspaper.

My time would be spent in a small bakery. The owner, Claire, was short staffed and welcomed my early arrival.

Artists new to the residency were paired with an established artist in their genre for one-on-one tutorial meetings. I was paired with a photographer named Dom.

The information I'd received told me he was no slouch. He had exhibited his work in the Museum of Modern Art, was collected by The Met and the Victoria and Albert Museum, and had produced five books. He was also on faculty at an exclusive private art school in California.

I knew much more about him than he knew about me, but it was all professional information. We knew nothing of one another personally.

ROMAN SKY

The most beautiful sky I'd ever seen was while walking over the Gianicolo in western Rome. It was so big. The city made great clouds. Giant. Bright white, heavy, and bloated with rain.

But this strange valley—hot, dry, and smeared with my memories—it did, on occasion, have a great sky. My second favorite. Especially during monsoon season.

I would miss the sky.

BAYONNE

It was Sunday. I ignored all that was going on in the house. The room went quiet as I read John Cheever's short story, *Bayonne*. I finished the story, soberly closed the book, and placed it on the coffee table.

It was a story about a woman in her early forties. She was a waitress in a blue-collar diner I believed to be in New York, although I don't know if he ever said this was so.

There was a sentence I could not shake. It described how one waitress felt before a younger waitress was hired and unknowingly stole her spotlight:

Her body then was unconsciously alive and vital, her eyes were bright and she smiled continually, the quiet, restrained smile of a woman walking in the power of men's admiration.

I read the sentence again, and again, and then once more.

DRIFTING

What I was seeking was more of a shape or state of being than something I could define with words. I think I believed I would find it and then return to my life, whole. Being whole was required. But *whole*, what does it really mean? Is it even possible? It is certainly different from existing as a fragment, but whether it is better or not depends on who you are asking, what sort of stakes are involved, and if they view the means as worthwhile.

This desire to return whole was something I figured out later. Everything appears clearer when looking back. My departure was actually a drifting light-headed sort of departure, like a dream, or being taken by the tide.

The girls were at school. Joe was at work. We'd all planned to meet at his Mother's house for dinner. I don't remember my taxi ride to the station, but clearly recall looking up at the giant schedule of departures, seeing my train would be leaving in fifteen minutes, and sliding my wedding ring into the front right pocket of my jeans.

THE STATION

The train pulls slowly to a stop. I tug my suitcase down from the rack above and exit into the blue hour. It is quiet. I can hear myself breathe.

The station is small with just one all-purpose shop. Scanning shelves, I see snow globes, candy bars, and cigarettes. I turn the wobbly rack of postcards until my eyes settle on a bold CALIFORNIA written across one of the cards, a barely noticeable *Greetings from* just above. I buy it, a stamp, and a small paper cup of coffee, and sit down on one of the smooth wooden benches in the empty waiting area.

I write *I love you and miss you* on the left, and our address on the right. I lick the stamp and press it against the card. It lands slightly crooked, but is still wet, so I slide it neatly into the corner. On my way out I drop the card into the station mailbox.

WHAT IS NECESSARY

The motel is beside the station. I walk. The night is hollow, my footsteps the only sound on the street.

My room has what is necessary. I undress, step into the shower, and am surrounded by pale pink tiles. I remove the tiny beige soap from its perfectly folded paper packaging and wash my tired self. A single white towel hangs from a bar on the wall. I dry off and slip beneath the sheets of my tightly made bed.

The coffee must have been weak. I'm already tired, exhausted. I don't feel at all like myself. And then, I am asleep.

TAKING NOTICE

I wake in the dark and pull the heavy curtain aside to reveal a parking lot and a few flickering street lamps. I stare out the window until the lamps go dark and the dull glow of natural light appears in the distance. The sun is beginning its rise.

I pull the curtain further, as far as it will go, and sit down on the bed. The depth and shape of everything within the frame of the window transforms as the sun reveals itself.

The sun rises, just like this, every single day, yet I cannot recall the last time I took notice.

ARRIVAL

I return to the station, buy another paper cup of coffee, a sugar donut, and board the train that will carry me along the next leg of my trip, the early train. It is filled with commuters. I am the only person toting luggage.

The train leaves the station and we soon enter a constructed landscape covered with large areas of black asphalt, tidy patches of green lawn, a few man-made ponds, three and five story office buildings, and narrow sidewalks weaving through it all. We stop often, commuters disembark, and bit by bit the train empties and grows quiet.

I fold my sweater, place it between my ear and the window, and lean against it. Then I close my eyes and let the sway of the train lull me to sleep.

After so many transfers I lose count, I am finally on the last leg of this journey, in a small bus. Perhaps it is more of a van, this small passenger vehicle the county calls *The Stage*. Once again, I drift off.

When I open my eyes I am squinting into the low sun and admiring green rolling hills dotted with black and white cows. Then I see horses, two deer, and, as I am informed by an elderly lady in the seat beside me, a *rafter* of wild turkeys.

I haven't seen an animal larger than a dog or cat since I left Chicago. The Lincoln Park Zoo. It reminds me of the girls. Why haven't I taken them to Chicago? They'd love that zoo.

No. You can't let your thoughts go there. Not yet, I think. And I work to shift my focus back to the cows and the sun.

The Stage arrives at my stop. I hesitate. *This is it. Can I do this?* I step down onto the pavement and reach into my left jacket pocket for the address, but it isn't there. I check the right. I know I put it in my left pocket the day before my departure, specifically so I wouldn't forget it. It's fine, I know it by heart, and I know it's just across the street from the stop, next door to the bakery.

It is dusk and quiet, but there is enough light for me to find my way. A man I swear is the Marlboro Man crosses my path, but I am sleepy. I let it go. I look up and see my new address beneath a porch light. I pause and set my suitcase down. I have a lemon tree. This is my porch, my light, my lemon tree. Home, for now.

MY COTTAGE

The first thing I see when I walk inside the cottage is the kitchen. It exhibits careful restraint. Nothing superfluous.

I take notice of the white eyelet curtains in the window above the sink. They look freshly washed. Someone cares about this place.

My table is made of beautifully worn wood planks, flush with character in the shape of knots, nicks, and circle stains from wet drinking glasses.

On the counter a dark crusty loaf of bread sits atop a weathered cutting board, an old knife rests beside it. There is also a mason jar with about an inch and a half of oil and a lid marked *olive* with black marker, a bamboo basket filled with small bright red strawberries, and a ceramic dish of moist coarse salt.

I taste a berry. It is sweet, really sweet.

Inside my refrigerator I find a second jar with a dollop of fresh ricotta inside, and a cold glass bottle of lemonade. I am thirsty and drinking straight from the bottle when I notice handwriting on a small scrap of paper on the table:

Thought you might be hungry, and thirsty.

Claire

FIRST DAY

I am woken by the sound of an unfamiliar alarm clock. It is 4:00 a.m.

Claire and I spoke briefly (she seems to gravitate toward brief) on the phone a few weeks ago. She said she would have most of her regular work out of the way before 5:00 a.m. and would then have some time to show me 'what's what.' I arrive just before 5:00.

I have forgotten to consider coffee—making or buying—so I go without. Claire hands me a cup as I walk into the bakery, easily, as if she's known me for years. She doesn't offer cream or sugar. She probably assumes anyone who agrees to work bakery hours drinks their coffee black. Luckily, I do. If I didn't, I'd change. There is something about Claire that makes me want to make her happy. She smiles for a moment after handing me the cup, but then gets right down to business.

Our main task is shaping bread dough into loaves. I watch her move quickly throughout the space, pointing and explaining. She is clear and succinct. Her wavy brown hair is tamed by a faded floral scarf. She wears an army green sleeveless t-shirt, jeans, and a utilitarian white apron. She looks hot, tired, and is covered in flour. But she moves with the grace and confidence of an off-duty ballerina. I like her.

SAINT ANTHONY

After work I decide to go to the market. I pick up a basket, but then just stand there, realizing I haven't shopped for one person in so long I've forgotten how. I muddle through.

When I get back to the cottage I place two bags of groceries on the table, walk back outside, and sit down at the top of the stairs. Why not? No one is waiting. It's just me. This perch allows me to look over the fence and onto the quiet action on the street. So there I sit, until I begin to feel hungry.

I pull two large beautifully beat up stockpots from the low cabinet beside the oven. The first I fill with water for pasta. I begin a sauce in the second. Olive oil and garlic first. I run outside and quickly cut a few fresh oregano stems from my garden and begin pulling the tiny leaves, forming a small pile on the cutting board. I assume this is how it is done. I usually use dried. My fingers smell green and good.

I open cans of whole tomatoes and crush each soft tomato in my hand before dropping it into the pot. I sweep half of the fresh oregano from the cutting board into the sauce and save the other half to add just before serving. Then salt and a pinch of sugar. I bring the sauce to a boil, stir it, and reduce it to a simmer, just as I recall my mother doing so many years earlier. Soon the whole place smells like home.

I can do this, I think. And then almost instantly, *No, I can't. This is crazy. I should go home.*

Motherhood is hungry. It takes what it needs. I let it transform me into something so basic and utilitarian, purely functional. I cannot exist as such. I need a path less narrow.

I blame no one. I've allowed this to happen. I'll fix it.

What is more important, a mother who is simply present, or a mother who searches for solutions, does not give in, and sets an example by following the beauty she sees in life?

The cottage doesn't have a television, but it does have two cases stacked with books. I find *The Temptation of Saint Anthony*. I like the title. Temptation and I have long been friends. I climb up to my little sleeping loft, turn on the lamp on my bedside table, crawl beneath the covers, and begin reading. I love the description of Saint Anthony's simple hermit's cabin. There is a loaf of black bread, a book, a knife, and little more. His sky has a pearl-gray tint. I feel a kinship with this man who wears a goatskin tunic and gazes upon the horizon.

THROUGH GLUE

I open my eyes slowly, and awake peacefully with the sun. Then, delayed a day, it hits me. My heart skips a beat and a sharp feeling of disorientation washes over me as I try to figure out where I am, and how I arrived. It is only my second morning and my sleepy mind is expecting to see the interior of my last residence, my home in the desert. My kids, my dirty dishes. Where has it all gone? The shock of what I have done comes crashing down on me.

The contrast of this punishment with the sunlight filtering in through the white eyelet curtains and the sweet sound of birdsong seems symbolic of the conflicting emotions with which I will have to learn to live, at least for the next year, perhaps longer. I know this is only a small fragment of the cross I will bear.

My body feels heavy as I force my legs over the side of the bed and place my feet on the floor. *You won't deal with this by going back to bed*, I think. *No, it won't happen. Those days are over. Get up.*

I drag myself into the bathroom, splash water on my face, and look up into the mirror. Thank goodness I'm not working today. I look tired. I think of all the smiles and frowns I've held over the years. The way expressions shape a face. Does the face of a person who experiences little emotion look younger? It doesn't matter. Inability to feel has never been an option for me.

My movements are slow, as if I am wading through glue, but I move forward. I brush my teeth, put on some lip gloss, and pull on a clean t-shirt and jeans. Stepping out into the crisp morning air, I walk briskly toward who knows where. It is my day off, I have time.

The where and why can come later. I just need to go. The glue slowly dissolves as I walk with deliberation right out of town, down the steps beside the bridge, and onto the trail by the creek. My head is held high, my shoulders back, and my breath strong and deep. A layer of fog rests just beneath the ridge, calmly, beautifully, and I hold on to that moment, like hands wrapped around a warm cup. I know I'll need it later.

ROUTINE

There is more waking in the dark, more shaping loaves, more grocery shopping, more time in my kitchen, more Saint Anthony, and more sitting on my top step.

I say hello to the cashier, Maria, before she rings up my groceries. She knows my name now, too. I learn the best coffee is brewed and sold in the feed barn, and bringing my own mug saves ten cents, and confirms I'm a local.

The bookstore posts upcoming events in their front window. Sometimes I take notes.

Summer Solstice Talk is written in black marker across the top of a flyer. The speaker is a *Visionary Activist Astrologer*. There will be a weekend workshop titled *Leaving the Village, Finding the Forest: Exploring the Soul and the Land in Poetry, Myth, and Music. A Fire Circle Performance* will take place Saturday, at 8:00 p.m.

Hmm, I think. *Not there yet.*

DOM

I like Dom, instantly. He is unpretentious, tells fabulous stories, and is comfortable to be around. He's taking a break from his regular teaching schedule and has relocated to the area to concentrate on his new body of work. He is exploring the history, landscape, and people of West Marin.

Working with my residency is his only other obligation. As suggested, we meet weekly. We discuss little of our projects and much of our lives, mostly our distant pasts.

I am waiting for Dom early one morning in the cafe, the only cafe. Shortly after I arrived in town a woman named Christine opened this cafe. She uses the same coffee beans they use in the feed barn, but rumor suggests Christine's coffee tastes richer and stronger. I don't agree, but she has a view of the bay. I am the first customer of the day and the cafe is quiet. I sit at a counter space and look out at the sunlight on the water.

When Dom arrives he sits down quietly beside me, places two mugs of hot coffee before us, and tells me the morning light is reminding him of Italy. He tells me how he was confused about what university life was offering him, and after his freshman year, at only eighteen years old, he'd decided to take a year off and travel. Dom arrived on the island of Salina that spring.

He'd heard he had family on the island, yet he hadn't met any of them, or confirmed where they might live. One hot day he arrived via cargo ship, carrying only a small satchel. He walked over to the bar beside the marina and explained his predicament, in broken

Italian, to the man behind the counter while ordering an espresso. Soon he was whisked into what still seems to him a fairy tale.

Apparently, his family members on the island had done quite well for themselves. His uncle sent a car to the bar to collect him and he was driven up through wildflowers and vineyards to a large stone house. He was greeted by his enthusiastic aunt and then shown by a maid to his cool room, fit with a large bed covered in crisp white sheets. He took a bath and had just put on the robe set out for him when his aunt practically danced into his room with a silver tray. The tray held a tiny cup of espresso, a bowl of sugar, a small spoon, and a glass of water. He got to know this tray well. His aunt adored doting on her newfound nephew and seemed to show up to confirm his comfort and offer him an espresso each time he paused to take a breath. He was treated like a king. She made it difficult for him to ever want to leave, but he did eventually begin to grow bored living in unearned privilege, and decided to return to America.

This is what meetings with Dom are like. He rarely notices the weather for the weather. It serves as a portal for him—the sun, a chill, the rain—they all take him to an earlier time and place.

DIPPED IN COFFEE

Claire is the only person I know, besides my mother, who dips her toast into her coffee. Should this mean something to me? Is it a sign of some sort?

The first time I see her exhibit this habit, I stare at her, dumbfounded. She is instantly annoyed and uncomfortable.

'What the hell has you so hypnotized?' she asks.

'Oh, sorry, it's just that, my mother, she's the only person I've ever seen do that.'

Claire does not ask me about my mother. She respects my privacy. This doesn't seem to be a place where people push and probe. They wait until you are ready, and if that means never, it appears to be fine.

ALTERED IMAGES

After much experimentation I confirm my least altered photographs
are the ones I most favor. Not the images exhibiting an unrelenting
focus on documentation, a replication of a scene precisely as it looks
outside the viewfinder, but a representation of my feelings in the
moment. Almost inevitably, such feelings are captured as I release
the shutter. There is little to gain by manipulation. It is nothing like a
poem.

COMFORT

I slouch lazily upon my sofa, feet up on the coffee table, hoping a comfortable pose will make me feel more comfortable inside, like smiling when you're not happy. It doesn't work.

So I bake. A loaf of white sandwich bread, with sesame seeds on top, the type my mom used to make. It helps.

BEFORE

One day the garden decides it is ready for me and invites me inside. I have waited patiently and kept a respectful distance as it mourned the loss of its former caretaker and good friend. Although we never met, I feel a certain kinship with her, and know I cannot take her place. This will be an adjustment for all involved.

The garden has taken on a life of its own, but its origins are still clear. It has not yet returned to wild. I trim the lavender and the rosemary, slightly, allowing each to dictate its general shape. The thyme remains low and requires little. The marjoram and mint seem rather selfish, but who am I to decide the power each plant should possess? I leave them to their politics. But I draw the line with the raised beds and remove everything but soil from each one. I have specific ideas for what each will hold. The chipped terracotta pots of geraniums will stay precisely where they were when I arrived, charmingly lining my steps.

A French woman was the last tenant to live in this cottage. Many of her belongings remain. In the kitchen hangs a list transcribed from a book by Marguerite Duras. It shows items she felt should always be in her country house. The difference between table salt and kitchen salt is not something I have formerly considered, but they are both on the list, two separate items. I am not sure how she differentiated one from the other, but I decide what each will be, for me. My table salt is fleur de sel and my kitchen salt is a coarse gray sea salt. Fleur de sel will dress slices of ripe tomato and quarters of cucumber. Coarse gray salt will be used in simmering soups and to season pasta water. Generally, gray for hot and fleur for cold.

The cabinets hold a small collection of mismatched porcelain, all rather feminine variations of blue and white.

Her silver looks gently used and comfortably elegant, just as I imagine her.

Several well-worn and dutiful linen tea towels, each with a double red stripe, are folded neatly inside the top kitchen drawer beside the sink.

My favorite cup's saucer has a flaw where it has been chipped. The flaw, very small, maybe an eighth of an inch in diameter, is located along the edge. I've gotten into the habit of caressing the flaw with my left forefinger while drinking tea.

Her pots and pans are heavy cast iron coated with various warm tones of enamel.

She was a writer who left Paris and came to the United States with an American man. *Paris. The girls would love Paris.* I tuck the thought away, saving it for later. No one I meet knows details of her life in Paris. They do know she lived with an American in Manhattan for a short time before retreating to this cottage to finish a novel she'd been unable to complete in New York. After being here only a few weeks, she sent the American a letter of apology and a request for her things. She lived alone in this cottage, continuing to write, for the rest of her life. The typewriter she used still rests on a high shelf in my closet. She sat before this fireplace on cold nights, made tea in this kitchen, sat at this table. Her presence is still strong, but never intrusive.

The allure of the cottage rests in both the cottage itself and the garden she cultivated. Both are lovely, yet sturdy, each able to hold their own alongside the rough and wild landscape of the coastline. The attraction is in the juxtaposition. Finding this special place in the world, a place that suits me so perfectly, and in a way I didn't even know I desired, seems too specific to dismiss as coincidence. Turning away would be ungrateful, but to whom I am unsure.

BIRDS

The sounds of suburban life are replaced mostly with the sound of birds. Birdsong. Something I hadn't given much thought. It is now a constant in my day, something to which I look forward.

STEALING GLANCES

I wake with the sun, no alarm. Today I know where I am. It is the first time I really stop and look out my loft window during daylight hours. The view over the wetlands, toward the ridge—it is magnificent.

Monday is the day of the week we rest, the only day we do not bake. Claire feeds her starter, but that is about it.

There is a yoga studio in the feed barn, separated from the coffee bar by the small room where vegetable seeds and pet food are stocked. I plan to attend my first class this morning, with Claire. Well, not actually with Claire, but I know she'll be there, and she knows my plans, too.

As I walk to class I notice the morning pace. It is special. It sweeps you away, but in a way opposite to what one might imagine when thinking of being swept away. It does so with its slowness rather than its speed.

I am early and decide to sit in the community garden and read while drinking my mug of coffee. I am happy to arrive in the studio before Claire. I've worried about whether I should set up my mat beside hers or further away so not to invade her personal space. She is very private, often curt, but also warm and kind. I don't want to make her feel uncomfortable.

The studio is small. Muted morning sunlight enters the space through a narrow horizontal window dressed in a sheer red curtain. The floor is made of wood, and warm. The instructor is quiet and calming. Claire arrives, gently places her mat beside mine, and nods in my direction. I nod in return and look down. Her feet are beautiful.

I continue to steal glances of them as I stumble through class. I hope she won't notice.

TOO MUCH

Since it is my day off and I have freedom with my schedule, I decide to take a bath, right in the middle of the day. My favorite time for baths. I soak while staring up at the ceiling, until my fingers and toes are shriveled and my mind is quiet, then I open the drain.

I like to lie still and wait for all of the water to leave the tub. On this day, the water stops draining when the tub is about half empty. I am so deliriously relaxed that it takes me a while to notice, but when I do, I delicately tap the drain with the big toe of my right foot and the suction begins again, briefly. I don't know how or where I learned this works. I tap again, and again, as needed, until the tub is empty and the porcelain cool.

I look at my shriveled fingers and think of what my father used to tell my sister and me about people who wash their hands too much. He did not specify how much was too much, but it was implied that Grandma, Mom's mom, fell into the too-much camp.

He told us incessant hand washers were trying to wash away something bad they had done, they felt guilty. Guilty of what, we didn't know. Again, he did not specify, he just left the word 'guilty' dangling in a way that made it seem especially dirty.

It's strange, the things in life one recalls. I wonder what he'd think of my long soaks in the tub.

SHIFTING WITH THE SUN

Claire does not structure her schedule around her family or her clients' demands. She works with the light. This is not a practical schedule for most people, but it suits me just fine. Claire likes to get her hands into the dough and start shaping loaves just as the light begins to filter through the trees and into the east windows. It is one of the most beautiful parts of the day, Claire would say *the* most beautiful, and early morning light adds such grace to this simple and quiet part of the bread baking process.

Our hours shift with the sun. Clients are flexible. They understand in a way that surprises me. They believe the calm and the pace inherent in this sort of baking makes the bread better. They say they can taste it.

THE MARLBORO MAN

I return home after work and sit on my top step, staring into the middle distance, pondering the pace in which years pass, and how that rate of passing appears to escalate with each new year. When we are children we don't think of such things, we live day-to-day. We are simply ourselves. There is no finding oneself, trying to get oneself back, or creating a new self. If I had one wish it would be to return to that state of mind, that pure presence, if only for a short while.

The breeze picks up, gently lifting strands of my hair and whirling them about. I am Medusa. Small twigs begin to skip across the crushed granite in my yard below. The Marlboro Man walks through my gate. *He's real*, I think. Not imagined, as I decided the night I arrived. I'm not sure if I am imagining him again or if he is actually standing before me, with a basket of strawberries.

No, I think, *the Marlboro Man most certainly cannot be standing before me with a basket of strawberries.* But he is. And I feel as if I've risen above the scene and become stuck, unable to return to the ground

'Hello,' he says to the woman with dancing hair. 'I'm Jack.'

I continue to look at him, my hair still whirling in the breeze, my mind still afloat, unsure if he is real or if my imagination has conjured him up to entertain me.

He continues, 'I know you are just getting settled in. I had a delivery for Claire and thought you might appreciate a little something to welcome you to the neighborhood. I have a berry farm nearby. We've just hit prime Seascape season. These are perfect.'

Still dazed, I take the berries. The basket is in my hand, the berries are real, so I surmise he must be real. I can't quite make it into the present, I'm still hovering just above and outside of it.

He breaks the silence with, 'Okay, now, well, have a nice afternoon.'

I still haven't said a word when he politely shuts the gate and waves goodbye.

Finally I whisper, 'Thank you,' into the empty yard.

TRIFLE

While considering what to do with the Seascapes I recall a strawberry trifle I learned to make when I was in high school. The recipe was in a *Good Housekeeping* magazine I flipped through while waiting in my dentist's office to have my teeth cleaned. It was one of those recipes that was actually an ad for one of the main ingredients. In this case, a partnership between JELL-O Pudding and Cool Whip. I glanced around the room, saw no one was looking, swiftly tore the page from the magazine, folded it twice, and stuffed it into my purse. I wanted the trifle to be my contribution to Joe's graduation party.

When I got back in touch with him, after all of those years, it was one of the first questions he asked me, 'Do you still make that layered strawberry whipped cream thing?' *No* was the truth, but I lied and said 'Yes.' The people with whom I'd surrounded myself over the last decade were not the JELL-O and Cool Whip type. I did once recreate the recipe with real heavy whipping cream, homemade custard, and Madagascar vanilla beans, but it wasn't the same. It didn't work. It was technically better, but it didn't taste of youth, and therefore felt a failure.

After a few dates with Joe I offered to make him dinner and surprised him with my original strawberry trifle for dessert. It worked. It took us both back in time, back to the period in our lives that came before adult sadness, serious responsibility, and all of the rougher spots life brings our way as we get older.

Per request, I made that trifle for just about every picnic, graduation, dinner party, and baby shower we attended over the last several
years, whether strawberries were in season or not. I learned to
despise it.

I rinse off the Seascapes and eat them straight from the basket.

We are quietly shaping when Claire says, 'So, you met Jack.'

'Mm-hmm,' I say.

'I use his Seascapes in the scones. He's a nice guy. His wife left him.'

'Did he deserve it?'

'No,' she says flatly.

I nod and we continue working.

Claire smiles and says, 'She was a bitch, and I thought so before she left him.' We both start laughing. It gets louder. A huge release, one it seems we both need. 'He's better off,' she says.

I nod again, and smile.

As we clean up, Claire wipes her hands on her apron and asks, 'Are you an alcoholic?'

'No,' I say.

'Okay, no judgments, we all have our demons, I just didn't want to ask you if you'd like a beer if you were. I have lemonade too. It's all the same to me. So, would you like a beer?'

'Sure.'

'An IPA?'

'Sure.'

'I'll meet you out front, on the chairs.'

We each recline in a faded red Adirondack chair and put our feet up on the large tree stump the chairs are angled toward. The sun is warm. The beer is cold. We both have a second beer, and as we're about midway through our third Claire looks out toward the street and says, 'I think he likes you.' And she pauses, a very long pause. I'm trying to gather my thoughts when she says, 'That's all I'll say. You don't have to respond. I just wanted you to know. He's a good catch. If I were available, I'd be interested.'

I feel like a junior high school girl. Smitten. I like it. 'Thanks for letting me know,' I say, with what I know is a goofy and embarrassed smile.

Claire stands up and says, 'I want pizza tonight, I definitely want pizza, homemade pizza. Do you want to take some dough home?'

'Yes.'

I get home and turn on the radio. Rick, the DJ, is playing jazz. It's perfect. I dance around my kitchen while making myself a pizza.

Sitting at my table, the radio's volume turned down to a hum, a cool breeze blowing through the window, I pause and admire my creation. Tomato, basil, and fresh mozzarella. That's it. I take a bite and it is everything I hoped it would be.

I hesitate about taking *Saint Anthony* to bed again. He's given me some very strange dreams. So I dust off *Excellent Women* and read myself to sleep.

START OVER

The morning sun streams in through the loft window and lands bright on my bed. A day off. I have no memory of what I read the night before. Oh well. I'll start over.

I squeeze a glass of orange juice and butter a slice of toast before climbing beneath a blanket on the sofa and returning to page one of *Excellent Women*. It's a funny book, very entertaining, but there is an underlying sadness stemming from Mildred's living alone—her eating half tins of baked beans without dignity, her preoccupation with other people's lives.

Should I be alone? I say it aloud and do not answer. I remain quiet, close the book, and place it on my lap.

RIDGE LIGHT

It is evening. I run up to the loft to put away my clean laundry and I am stopped by the light. The sun is already behind the ridge, leaving a thin pastel film over everything except the cypress trees. They are dark and majestic. They do not succumb. The contrast is striking.

I forget about the laundry, prop my pillow up against the head-board and lean back into it, my legs extended in front of me, and watch the light change. The sky is a washed out blue. Darkness slowly fills in the details of the landscape and soon the ridge is a mere silhouette. The blue of the sky deepens and the foreground disappears. Then it is night.

THE KNIT STITCH

After work one day I decide to rummage around in the shed. Claire
has told me she has no idea what is buried inside and I am welcome
to whatever I find. Beneath a few moving blankets and a layer of
dust I discover an old potter's wheel, the type you spin with a kick. I
pull it out onto the cracked concrete driveway in front of the shed,
find a couple of rags, and start cleaning it. I scrub every crevice until
it shines.

Claire stops by to ask if she can steal a few lemons from the tree.

'It's your tree,' I tell her.

'Not anymore.'

'Well then, of course, steal as many as you like.'

'Ah, the old wheel. I don't even recognize it. Astrid will have clay.
You'll meet her at the knitting group tonight.' She plucks a few
lemons from the tree and she's gone.

Yes, the knitting group. 4:30. I'm reluctant, but I need to meet
people. *I need more than Claire, Dom, and books in my life*, I think.
Actually I'm not really sure what I need. Maybe I don't need more.

I hope I'm not an intrusion. Claire claims people drop in and out
each week and it isn't a big deal. She tells me everyone is welcome.

In town I buy a skein of cream-colored cotton yarn and a set of
handmade needles. I roll my yarn into a ball, cast on, and knit a few
rows before leaving for the library.

I didn't pack the needles Mom gave me when Dad was in the hospital. It didn't occur to me that I might knit here.

Mom only taught me to cast on and the simple knit stitch, but it was all I needed. I remember being enamored with the first little square of fabric I produced. Mom told me to just knit knit knit until it looked a length I liked for a scarf and then I could worry about finding someone to help me cast off.

There was something soothing about the monotony of knitting the same stitch, over and over. The feeling of the yarn moving through my fingers, the act of watching something take shape, right there in my own hands. It was fortifying.

I struggled when Mom first tried to teach me the simple knit stitch. I was clumsy and distracted, but eventually caught on. I think she enjoyed teaching me something, sharing one of her skills with me. She was the instructor, and I the innocent, completely helpless and dependent on her.

She didn't mention it, but she must have been aware of the power of the yarn and those needles. I needed them. I knit a simple pale blue scarf that winter. It was and is my favorite scarf. When I wrap it gently around my neck I'm instantly comforted.

I recall that time so clearly, sitting up with Dad at night, keeping him company. He hated being alone during that period. It was just the two of us and I was stiff with worry, the weight of his world resting heavily on my shoulders. Each night I'd wait for him to fall asleep in his chair, pick up my knitting needles, and allow my mind to rest in the repetition. Knit stitch after knit stitch, no variation, ever. It was the one stable thing.

I continued knitting after Dad recovered, but hadn't moved on to more complex projects. What I enjoyed was the *act* of knitting. The finished project was a by-product.

I wonder how experienced the women in the group will be. Then I think, *whatever*. I have a conversation topic to distract from my amateur knitting—my newfound pottery wheel.

When I walk into the library the large rectangular table closest to the door has several women sitting around it. No men. There are baskets, books, yarn, and needles. The women seem content, but fairly serious about their craft. No aimless chatter. No laughter. I'd kind of hoped for both.

I approach the table and open my mouth, nervously. Out comes something close to a whisper, 'I assume this is the knitting group. Room for one more?' I smile and look down, a little off to the side.

'Of course, sit down,' says the woman at the head of the table. She seems in charge. 'My name is Sam. Welcome. What do you have there? The beginning of a scarf? It looks a fine wool.' I'm about to correct her and tell her my yarn is cotton when I remember Mom mentioning some knitters, usually older ladies, refer to all types of yarn as *wool*. It seems Sam is one of these knitters. She is strong and sure. There is wisdom in her voice. I'm not mentioning cotton.

I knit and observe, quietly. All knitting questions are directed toward Sam. Her answers do not disappoint.

The middle-aged woman to my left introduces herself to me. Her name is Astrid. She tells me she is the bad girl in town and winks her left eye. I assume her wink implies irony, but I'm not sure. 'What brings a nice young woman like you to a place like this?' she asks.

'Bread, and photography,' I answer.

'Fair enough. Glad to have you.' She doesn't pry. No one does. I am relieved. The yarn and the company feel good and the hour ends too quickly.

It is precisely 5:30 when Sam, the woman I determine to be the matriarch of the group, pops up and says, 'I must get home to Henry.' It seems there is more to the statement, something everyone but me knows. I am an outsider. No one knows me. It is fair. I don't mind.

I finish my row, say goodbye to the other women, and then browse the stacks for a while. I find a book outlining the history of knitting and a beginner's how-to pottery book. I decide to get a

library card. On my way to the librarian's desk I realize I've forgotten
to ask Astrid about clay, and when I turn around the table is empty.
A tidy and efficient group, they have all gone.

TOWN POTTER

The next day, on my way home from the market, I open the gate and spot a large plastic bag filled with a block of pale gray on the mat before my door. There is a note wedged beneath the lower right corner:

Claire mentioned you were experimenting with the old wheel. Warning—This clay might be older than the wheel. Drop it in a bucket of water and soak it for a while.

See you Thursday,
Astrid.

Once inside the cottage I jot down a note to myself:

Thursday - lemons as a thank you for Astrid.

I walk back outside with my camera and sit on the top step. It is my favorite time of day, the hour or so after sunset. I look through the viewfinder and pan slowly to the right, then the left. What I want is just off center, slightly to the right to include the lemon tree, the lens barely tilted down. I press the shutter release.

The post of town photographer is taken, but I don't mind. Photography is not something I see as a career. My inspiration is unpredictable. Attempting to harness it would surely wear away what is natural and good.

Could I be the town potter? Is there such a thing? *Why not*, I think. It's a lovely utilitarian title. A pure and honest existence, serving my community.

Why shouldn't one try on different futures, like hats? Assumptions are always a bad idea. Trials are required.

I could split my time between the bakery and my wheel. Bread and clay. Baker and potter. Mugs, bowls, and loaves of crusty bread. I'd sign the bottom of each piece of damp pottery with a dull pencil and score my bread baker's signature into the top of each loaf of bread. Centuries from now archeologists will unearth Claire's brick oven. I'm not sure how they'll know who baked, but they'll find fragments of pottery with my signature and discover I was the town potter.

SLATE BLUE

It is one of those heavy deep slate blue days, the type I begin beneath a weight. The air feels eerie and damp. I put on my jacket and scarf, sling my camera around my neck, and head out the door. It is early and the street is empty. I walk toward the creek. The weight hangs over my shoulders and trails heavily behind me. I march through town ignoring it, hoping it will go away.

After about a mile and a half it lifts. Still, I imagine it close and ready to return. I fear any sign of weakness will be seen as an invitation.

I end up beside the creek, surrounded by green. I slump down on a patch of dirt, watch the water and bits of debris pass, and begin to cry. I don't try to stop, I just let it happen.

Soon the tears subside and I walk to a flat grassy area, lie down, and look straight up at the sky, now a blue more Egyptian than slate. The air has warmed. The clouds are white and few. They move slowly, stretching and changing shape as they pass. I look through the viewfinder and wait for a moment of cloudless pure blue.

MATT

I can feel his eyes on me as I cross the street for my coffee. There he is, as always, reclined in an Adirondack chair just to the right of the feed barn entrance. His mannerisms and smile are mischievous. I've never heard him speak a word. He always looks slightly wounded yet amused by my avoidance. I think he likes it.

His stance is so patronizing, comical even, like he knows I'll come around and eventually be taken by his charm. There is something about him that makes me believe he might love me, just a little, like he is the type that can do so from afar, the type who can know someone just by looking into their eyes. I buy my coffee and wait to turn the corner before smiling.

LIBRARIES

I've always felt protected in libraries—secure, comfortable. I like going alone. Early. When the librarian has just unlocked the door, before she turns on the lights. There is a heavy calm created by the near silence and the time the books have been alone with themselves. We move about slowly, careful not to disturb the mood, until the phone rings or the doorknob turns, and everything changes.

RAIN

I tell Claire I need to drive. She hands me her keys and tells me to head southwest toward the ocean, that I'll stumble upon a town she thinks I'll like.

'Don't look for signs, there won't be any,' she says. 'If you run into the beach you've gone too far. Try to act comfortable, not too conspicuous. They don't like outsiders.'

I say, 'Okay,' hesitantly. 'And I'll like it?'

'It sounds worse than it is. Just go.'

So I go. It is drizzling and the fog is thick. I drive too far, end up by the beach, and park the truck.

The Pacific Ocean. It is rough, nothing pacific about it. I stand and look out at it for a while. I can taste the salt when I lick my lips. The whitecaps seem to go on forever, well beyond the horizon line. I envy the Pacific. Its air of infinite possibilities, its vast space to make up for each mistake and try something new.

I walk back up the road and find a library. It is warm. I am cold and wet. I look around, pick up a few books, then sit down and read a page here, a page there, hoping my clothes will at least begin to dry.

As I'm leaving I hear the librarian say, 'Perfect day for soup at the cafe,' to no one in particular. She's daydreaming and looking out the window. I am the only other person in the library, so I ask, 'I could really use some soup, where's the cafe?'

She directs me out the door, through the parking lot, a couple of blocks down, on the right. A white building with yellow frames

122

around the windows. The actual name of the cafe escapes her. 'I'm not sure it has a name,' she says. 'You'll know.'

And I do. It has old wood plank floors and walls, and is decorated like a fishing cabin with hints of surf hut. There is a pot bellied stove burning in the corner. I sit beside it. Split pea with ham, served with a chunk of Claire's bread, and a pint.

SHAPING

Morning light. A landscape still and sleeping. Dew glistening and drawing my attention to spider webs I swear did not exist the day before. They seem to have been woven in the night. So many of them. I stop to breathe it all in.

I almost believe these mornings, this landscape, this rhythm of shaping these smooth elastic balls of dough into loaves could become my life. It is quiet, dependable, and leaves my mind free to wander. I nestle into the routine. It gives no resistance. Each day like the day before, except for new webs, and the way the sun shifts with the seasons.

HAND BUILDING

For some reason, the pottery wheel and I are at odds. It does not offer the bliss I had anticipated, but the slab roller has become my friend. I much prefer the peaceful pace of rolling out a slab of clay and hand building my pots and plates over the targeted pressure, strength, and timing required by the wheel.

I eventually push the wheel back into the corner of the shed and focus my attention on the slab roller. I begin to understand the old butcher-block table I use for wedging air bubbles from clay and shaping slabs, the drying shelves, and the kiln, but there is still a lot about clay I do not understand. I enjoy the experimentation, and accept the failures.

CLEARING

The sun is heavy and low. Little light remains in this day, yet as I sit and look down into the yard I cannot help but feel overcome with an urge to clear space. There is an odd little patch of soil, lush with an array of weeds. I've become comfortable calling it *The Amoeba*. I have a vision of it bursting with bright green baby lettuces.

I decide it is time. I pop up, head inside, and put on the long sleeve shirt and hat I picked up at the thrift shop for gardening. Then I burst back out the door and begin pulling weeds from *The Amoeba*. It is like leaving the present and entering some sort of vacuum, everything but the weeds falls away.

The space is cleared fairly quickly and almost obsessed, I move on to the former duck cage, where I plan to trellis peas. I have only ever eaten frozen peas. I have not even seen them in fresh pods. I am looking more forward to the shelling than the eating, the type of shelling you see in old movies and television shows, the type where three generations sit on a sprawling front porch, in wooden rocking chairs, quietly shelling, while a cousin gently strums an old guitar, a pitcher of lemonade nearby.

The cage is full of rough thorny vines and the work requires large clippers, takes twice as long to clear, and brings me that much more satisfaction. When I finish it is dark.

I walk inside, take off my hat, and look into the hall mirror. I am breathing heavily. There are dried leaves and small twigs tangled in my hair. My cheeks are pink.

CONTROL

Spending time in the yard here has me thinking back to my time in Dad's front and back yards, just after his surgery. I had many new behaviors emerge during his recovery. The mind and body are resourceful in their creation of defense mechanisms.

Each day I was driven outside. I gathered mounds of pomegranates, fallen and rotten, and deposited them into his compost pile. I meticulously weeded the front yard and then walked back and forth, slowly, scanning every inch for discarded cigarette butts, gum wrappers, or any other remnant of street rubbish. The space would remain pristine, for at least a day or two, and then I'd begin again.

There were the flowering sage bushes in Dad's front yard, flowers absent. He told me they flowered after the rain. I couldn't wait for the rain, so I soaked the bushes every evening and darted out front each morning to see if any of the tiny purple flowers had appeared.

And there was the sad, limp, and neglected basil plant I coddled, hoping to bring it back to life. I watered it gently and often, moved its pot around the front porch throughout the day for optimal sun exposure, and removed all dead leaves and debris from its base area so it could breathe more easily.

It was years ago, yet I'm just now realizing I must have been searching for something I could control. I needed to believe I could make a difference, improve a life, any life, in the midst of such disarray.

SOUNDTRACK

My cottage has old windows that shake within their frames when the wind picks up. Birdsong along with this dull heavy rattle is the soundtrack behind most of my early mornings and late evenings.

I like it. Complete silence makes me nervous.

LEMONADE

I take a glass and bottle of lemonade outside and sit down on the top step. Jack walks by. I see him. He does not see me. I pause for a minute and then jump up, run inside, slip on my sandals, take a quick reckless look in the mirror, pat my cheeks to bring up a little color, put Vaseline on my lips, grab a measuring cup, and dart down the steps, tripping on the last, but recovering rather well.

Soon I am on the street in front of my cottage exhibiting complete poise and calm. I watch Jack open Claire's gate and walk inside. I open it about two minutes later. They are still in the yard, just outside the bakery.

He must be about 6' 2". He looks perfectly fit in his plaid shirt and Wrangler jeans. Strong and comfortable, yet humble and polite. There is something about him that makes me believe he has time traveled here from an earlier, more well-mannered era. Such a beautiful man. And I don't think he knows it.

I snap out of my daydream when I notice them noticing me and say, 'Oh. Hi. I don't want to interrupt, just want to borrow a little sugar so, um, I can make some lemonade.' I try hard not to think of the full bottle of lemonade I just left on my step, and the five pound bag of sugar in my cabinet.

Claire, although she already knows the answer, asks, 'Have you two met?'

We both say 'Yes' at the same time. Then I say, 'Okay,' for no reason at all, hurry into the bakery, fill my measuring cup with sugar, and then blurt out, 'Okay, thanks bye,' and make my quick exit, leaving a trail of sugar on the way. *Oh my,* I say to myself as I move swiftly back to my cottage. *What the hell was that?* I put the sugar down on the counter and take a deep breath.

PRECISELY AS I AM

What is most interesting about Dom is the way he sees other people. I don't know how he does it. He does not look at those around him through the filter of his own experience. When he shares his opinion with me I know he has placed his history aside to see me precisely as I am.

One day we are chatting. I am telling him a story and he stops me midway through and asks, 'Have you ever thought of writing a book?'

I say 'No, I haven't.' But as I answer the question I can see it happening, someday.

I walk all the way to Christine's for coffee, slowly, a distance I usually choose to drive. I know he'll be at my usual coffee spot and I can't face him, not yet. I need to walk, to clear my head.

I remove *The Sea, The Sea* from my tote bag and open it close to the beginning, where my bookmark rests. Charles is describing his anchovy paste on hot buttered toast. *This is much better*, I think. I needed a break from *After Leaving Mr. Mackenzie* and the sad Julia Martin holed up in her cheap Parisian hotels, so I left her on the table beside my bed. After vacillating between reading the same anchovy toast description over and over and gazing out the window at the bay, I finally close the book and simply gaze.

When gazing ceases to be enough, I leave the cafe to move closer to the bay, and sit on a big old log resting beside the water. The sun is breaking through the morning fog, creating a thin line of glimmering light in the distance.

I don't know who I am anymore. It isn't an empty statement. I've lost track. I still have my plan. Getting myself together, developing a stronger self, and then returning to my real life. But that real life is fading and this one, the one that felt so alien to me at first, is beginning to feel like the real one.

Looking down, I watch a small patch of sunlight land upon my feet. It is warm. I drift back to the day before yesterday.

It is an unseasonably warm day. After work I decide to stop by the feed barn, buy some pea seeds, and then visit the bookstore. The bookstore is an amazing place, there is something magical about it. Whenever I enter I feel as though the space has been drawn around me, a perfect fit. It is always quiet, quieter than the library, and I like the way the woman at the counter pauses and lovingly runs her hand over each book I purchase before placing a bookmark inside.

I leave the bookstore with Jean Rhys and her tales surrounding Mr. Mackenzie. It has been a while and I feel like reading it again. Sitting down on the bench in front of the store, I open the book. Soon I am transported back to 1920s Paris, seeing through the eyes of a young woman who feels old. It is a landscape both beautiful and dark:

"She found pleasure in memories, as an old woman might have done. Her mind was a confusion of memory and imagination. It was always places that she thought of, not people. She would lie thinking of the dark shadows of houses in a street white with sunshine; or trees with slender black branches and young green leaves, like the trees of a London square in spring; or of a dark-purple sea, the sea of a chromo or of some tropical country that she had never seen."

And I am jolted back into the present when he sits down beside me, cold six-pack in hand, and slyly says, 'Hello.'

It is Matt. He speaks. There isn't anything humble or gracious about him. He is sure and determined and carries both with ease. He is the opposite of Jack. His usual knowing smile is drawn wide across his handsome face.

He recognizes my book, shakes his head and says, 'Oh, that's a dark one, but not her darkest.'

I look at him strangely. He's either read After Leaving Mr. Mackenzie and is familiar with at least one other Jean Rhys novel or is unbelievably adept at pretending to have done so. I want to believe him.

He spots the packet of pea seeds I have resting beside me and tells me he's started his a few weeks ago. He asks if I have a trellising plan and tells me he's created a genius structure. He'd be happy to show me, if I'm interested. I know I should not be interested.

Next thing I know I am in the front seat of his shabby little pickup truck, windows down, my hair blowing in the breeze, six-pack between us. 'No clouds,' he says. 'Considering the sliver of waning moon I saw last night, the stars should own that sky tonight.'

I don't even know what to say. Who is this guy?

The ride is strikingly beautiful. He lives in a small glass house. The view from his sofa is hypnotic. Mounds of pale pink wild roses with golden rolling hills as a backdrop. He offers me a beer, and then another. Soon we are into his record collection and taking turns playing DJ. One more beer. I haven't had this much fun since college and soon forget anything resembling inhibitions. I do not see the trellised peas. I do see a gorgeous dusk sky. And later what I believe to be my first truly dark night. A moon so slim it is barely visible. I've never seen a sky so black and stars so white.

He drops me off at the bakery the next morning, in yesterday's clothes. I'm only five minutes late. Claire doesn't seem to notice the five minutes, or my clothes.

I look back out at the bay, the fog has cleared, and I can feel the sun crawling up my legs, my stomach, up onto my shoulders, and finally across my face. I soften as the chill melts. As I turn away from the bay, I see Jack's truck pass.

It is small, this one evening of indiscretion, in the whole scheme of things, in this life I've lived so far, and all I have yet to live. Very small. I've done much worse. So I walk back toward the cottage along the shoulder of the road, beside the woods, looking into the trees, and then across the street toward the bay, the rolling hills in the background. I kick a rock, and another, a pinecone, and when I look up I see her.

Sunlight has found its way through the dense treetops and it looks as if a spotlight has been summoned to rest upon her. A mermaid. She is poised, relaxed, and holds a gentle expression. Such grace. As I get closer I see she is life-size, carved from wood, and appears to have been painted long ago.

No photographs. It feels wrong to move any closer, intrusive, so this is all the detail I see. She does not seem lost or in need of assistance. What is she doing here? I stand at a respectful distance and admire her, wondering if she is really here, if I am awake; and if she is here and I am awake, will she still be here tomorrow? I hope so. She is magical and I want to get to know her. I'll move slowly.

UNFOLDED

My mind has completely unfolded. I had to move it from my small living room floor out into a nearby meadow. It requires space, like a giant map. The meadow is large enough to let every wrinkle, each tight crease, rest flat.

Reading it is strange. I've grown accustomed to the stress of folding and unfolding, never enough time or space to complete either. Now the individual thoughts are free, each existing in its own area. I follow the winding blue line and find my YOU ARE HERE.

It is all so clear, but what they don't tell you is there is always an adjustment period, even when moving into clarity. I thought additional space yielded simplicity, and perhaps in some ways it does, but it is not what you'd imagine. The openness, the space for all of it to be accessible at once. The clean idea of it is different than the reality. I feel more exposed than comforted.

WISH YOU WERE HERE

I climb into the claw foot tub and sink down in the clear warm water. Soft shafts of light enter through the small square window above and reach diagonally toward the floor, resting on the bath mat. I feel relaxed, sleepy, and drift off into one of those half-awake half-asleep states of mind. The type where your thoughts feel like those of a narrator rather than your own.

She stepped quietly through his front door and walked toward the guest bedroom. The cool morning air had gone and the house was hot. She struggled out of her jacket and tossed it on the bed.

Her father slept while she rummaged through his hall closet and located their family photos. She moved through them quickly. She wanted to find a specific photo her father had taken of her and her girls, and time was running out. She'd be gone before dinner tomorrow.

She stumbled upon a postcard. Out of the entire box, there was only one picture postcard. It was addressed to her and her sister.

During the winter holidays of her tenth year, her sister's seventh, her father escaped to Florida with his mistress. His handwriting exhibited such casual spacing and grammar. It was obvious he found the whole ordeal minor and quite forgivable.

Hi! Guys.

I miss you wish you were here.
I'm sorry I missed you for Thanksgiving but I'll see you as soon as I
get home.

Love Dad

His tone. She hated and envied it at the same time.

*Thanksgiving was a very big deal in her family. How could he not have
seen this? Her mother showed up for the big family dinner with her and her
sister in tow. They dined with her grandmother and the families of her
father's six brothers and sisters. Everyone knew why her father wasn't
present. No one asked questions.*

*What she didn't understand was how that postcard had stayed with him
through the decades. How it got into that box. Who packed it? How was it
the only piece of mail in this box of photographs? So many of her treasured
diaries, works of art, and letters had disappeared, yet somehow this postcard
remained in her father's house. You'd think it would be something he'd
rather see burned, but no, he just wasn't like that.*

I drain the tub and remain reclined and cradled in the strength of
porcelain over cast iron. Concession drifts into the room and drapes
itself over my warm wet skin.

When the heat finally leaves my body I get out of the tub, wrap
one towel around my body, and a second around my wet hair. I pull
my suitcase from beneath my bed, unzip the outside pocket, and
remove the postcard. I sit down on the sofa and hold it up to the
lamplight, looking at the ridiculous faded image of the sponge diver
on the front of the card, and my dad's happy handwriting on the
back. It was a long time ago.

THE MARKET

It is the first day of the season for the farmers market. Jack arrives early. He looks rugged and exquisitely handsome. It does not go unnoticed. Women turn into silly little girls around him and he does nothing to draw this forth. They all blush in his presence. It doesn't matter what he says, it seems the female response is always smiling, nodding, and touching his shoulder—any excuse to touch his shoulder.

Jack sets up his table and begins arranging baskets of strawberries, taking a quick break to walk over to the coffee bar and order a cup of black coffee.

Astrid and I decide to visit the market together. We meet at the coffee bar. A local pastry chef and friend of Astrid's has decided to serve her experimental donuts this morning. She's been toying with some new ingredients—Jack's strawberries, another farm's apricots, cardamom, star anise, Earl Grey tea, and dark chocolate. We are waiting patiently when Astrid's friend walks up with a tray of warm donuts and a soft smile.

She lets us select one donut each before displaying the rest in the coffee bar's glass case. I choose a chocolate star anise. Astrid reaches for an apricot cardamom glaze. As we melt into puddles of delight, Jack walks up, snatches a strawberry Earl Grey, takes a bite, and stomps his foot like an anxious horse, rolling his eyes in delight, and is offered another.

No one really knows Jack and it seems they don't mind. They are happy just looking. It is strange to see a man draw so much attention

and at the same time exude such loneliness. Maybe it is the loneliness
that attracts them. It makes me uncomfortable.

THE SHED

The shed is becoming something else. Much more than a shed. I swept out the corners and dusted, working until each shelf and piece of furniture was ready for a new beginning.

I mop one last time, and move on to the windows. I polish them with newspaper and vinegar until I remove every trace of fingerprint, dust, and all haze the raindrops have left behind.

Pottery equipment is arranged near the door, where I've been working. The old desk and chair face the large paned window. I place my journal and pencil on the center of the desk.

I sit down, facing the window, and watch as the last of the day's sunlight begins fading into darkness. Then I jump up and grab my camera. I press myself into the back wall and look through the viewfinder, hoping to capture as much of the scene as possible, before the light changes.

LET'S GO

I watch him tear open two crusty rolls and layer a few thick slices of salami atop the lower halves. He then walks out the back door and quickly back into the kitchen with a handful of arugula leaves he places atop the salami. He drizzles a grassy green olive oil over the arugula, and then tops the oil with some coarse ground pepper. That's it. I know it will be delicious. He places a blanket, the sandwiches, and two cold bottles of beer into a canvas bag and says, 'Let's go.'

We drive up into a hidden neighborhood I didn't even know existed. Houses are tucked behind large trees and carved into cliff faces. We park alongside the road and follow a winding dirt path down to a little crescent shaped beach that reminds me of one I found in Italy long ago, in Portofino.

He spreads the blanket out over the sand on the far side of the small beach, in a shady area beside a cliff. There is a family enjoying themselves on the other side of the crescent, but the echo of the waves off the cliff muffles all but the sounds of distant laughter. Matt has this way of orchestrating moments I want to live in, forever.

BETWEEN THE DOING

The quiet moments, between the doing. They are difficult. But necessary for growth.

I invite them.

NEW AGAIN

It is early. I open my eyes and smile, remembering my plans for the day. Monday. No yoga. No work.

Crusty bread, sharp cheese, tart apples, water, and a blanket are placed inside my tote bag. I quickly get dressed, pull my hair up into a ponytail, and am on my way.

When I open my door all I can see is fog. As I move forward, various objects come into view. First the top of the stair rail, then the first step, soon the latch on the gate. I walk onto the street, only making out shapes of muted color with fuzzy edges. A beautiful blur. The air feels so clean. I breathe deeply. It is quiet. I don't even hear birds. It seems I am the only creature awake.

The plan was to spend the entire day lounging on the beach. I expected sun. But I will not let fog and a chill stop me. I'll adjust. I walk cautiously along the right side of the road to the beach trail. As I make my descent the fog begins to fade. The air warms.

I meander down the hill, through the brush and beneath the trees, before emerging onto quiet empty beach. Seated on my blanket I look out across the bay, read, eat, and eventually fall asleep beneath the sun.

When I wake it is dark, a giant amber moon resting in the water before me. It's magnificent, the largest moon I have ever seen. Everything around me glows golden.

I wrap myself in my blanket, use my rolled up tote bag as a pillow, and spend the night.

The next morning I walk barefoot on the cool sand, each step massaging my feet. The rising sun warms my face. When I reach the edge of the bay I slip out of my clothes and wade into the clear cold water. An array of sharp tiny bumps form on my tightened skin. When the water reaches my thighs I bend my knees and spring forward, making a shallow dolphin-like dive beneath the water.

Still submerged, I stretched my arms forward and then wide, moving through a breaststroke, surfacing for a breath, and squinting into the sun.

I am new again.

SLOWLY

I still don't know much about Matt. I want the knowing to come slowly. Slowly is always more gratifying.

I know he lives in a small glass house with a wood deck. A quiet place. An odd little estate protected by a perimeter of tall wild rose bushes, atop a grassy hill.

He likes Jean Rhys, old records, beer. And me, I think.

TOMATO AS JAM

Olive oil now serves as butter, tomato as jam. I eat Claire's bread toasted, with olive oil, a sweet fat tomato sliced thick, fleur de sel, and coarse ground pepper. The ripe slices almost melt on warm toast. I eat the sections of tomato that do not fit on my toast while leaning over the sink, juices dripping, as I would a ripe peach.

THE GLASS HOUSE

Matt does not know when the glass structure he calls home was originally built, or what purpose it served. The county holds no record of its original building permit. It seems a fragment of something larger, perhaps the small orangerie of an estate swallowed by an earthquake. It does lie directly beside the San Andreas Fault.

The property was vacant for so long no one recalled it ever being otherwise. In fact there was not a soul living in the area who'd even known the glass structure existed on the property before it was put up for sale. The natural landscape had long ago taken over and obscured it from view.

The little house, a misshapen rectangle, not quite a parallelogram, is lined on three sides with large sturdy panes of old wavy glass. Several panes in the top row of each of the three walls pull open by latch, tilting diagonally. The floor is made of uneven stone, the old roof is slate. The fourth wall is solid and looks as if it covers what could have once been the entrance into another structure.

There was no electricity or plumbing when Matt purchased the property, but he remedied the situation and constructed a small kitchen and bath. The space is odd and beautiful, somewhat haunting, yet I feel cradled when I am there, protected.

WHISPER

We pick blackberries for breakfast and drop them whole into our pancake batter. The berries soften as the batter browns and crisps around the edges and we serve the cakes with generous pats of butter melting on top. Hot mugs of sweet milky coffee rest beside our plates.

After breakfast we walk into the fog, beside the tule elk. We see a female first, just her head, emerging from the fog. Walking just a few more steps reveals fourteen additional female and calf elk standing all around her. It is a spectacular site. Further along we see two male elk, each sporting enormous antlers. Matt sweet-talks them, quietly, as we pass, hoping they are in good spirits.

The fog does not break, it holds all ten miles of our hike. So beautiful, everything hushed. We walk softly and whisper the entire day.

Things are moving beyond one night of indiscretion. I don't care.

DEPTH

Gravenstein apples disappear in early September. I try to replace them with McIntosh, but in comparison they taste like lemons. I move on to Green Golden Delicious and they fall flat. I like the way their skin snaps when I bite into them, but their flavor lacks depth, and what good is anyone or anything without it?

FOCACCIA

Claire sells out of bread consistently and wants a new challenge, but not too big of a challenge. Something simple. She asks me what I think. I suggest focaccia. She likes my idea.

I feel as if I've made it through some sort of initiation. Ah, the contentment. Claire likes my idea.

SNOW ANGEL

I walk outside and into the early morning air. The sky is white with faint gray smudges. It is silent with the exception of a passing breeze rustling a few crisp dead leaves. The rustle slows to a stop and I am enveloped in quiet. Tiny droplets of water float through the air, slowly, before landing on my face. So light, like snow, bringing back childhood memories of winters in Chicago. They are recollections so drenched in nostalgia they cannot be matched in real life.

Waking up and looking out our living room windows onto a landscape dusted with pristine white. I am five years old.

I am flat on my back on our snow-covered front lawn, giggling and waving my arms and legs madly, leaving the imprint of an angel.

Pushing my mittens down inside my coat pockets and freeing my tiny bare hands to gather up a handful of soft cold snow and packing it tightly into an icy ball.

And my favorite part of winter, the thin layer of white, blanketing the topside of every branch and fragile twig of the naked trees lining my street.

I return to that time, fully, free from all that has taken place since then—my lies, my mistakes, my regrets. They are gone. It's just me, on my snow-covered lawn. A tiny angel.

THE STRANGER

As Camus wrote in *The Stranger*:

after a while you could get used to anything

Is it true? Could I return home, move to Lapland, stay here and work in the bakery? Would I adjust equally to any scenario?

A WOODPECKER'S WORK

I look up and see thousands of tiny holes blanketing the Douglas fir before me, many of those holes housing acorns. A woodpecker's work.

They understand their talent, they know their path. Simple lives, fully mapped, but choiceless.

What would happen if one of the woodpeckers were handed a train ticket and sack of cash?

PERFECT

Sunday has become our day for experimenting. We decide to move forward with focaccia. Our goal, to create a product that speaks of our hands, Claire's brick oven, and West Marin. We begin with a basic rosemary, olive oil, and sea salt focaccia. There is discussion of trying other ingredients such as garlic, caramelized onions, and plum tomatoes later, but I kind of know we won't.

Our first batch is near perfect, exactly what we had in mind. We stand quietly, proudly, side by side, admiring our work. Not a word is spoken, the only sound is our satisfied breath. The air in and around the shop smells of rosemary. It is still dark outside. We don't test other ingredients, we don't change a thing.

As the sun rises I walk around the corner and deliver a modest tray to the retail bakery. Our first focaccia. We are curious to see how people will respond. The bell on the bakery door jingles and I assume, this early, it is an employee, but it isn't.

It's Dad.

Obviously, I can't see myself, but I imagine I turn white. Dad waltzes in with the same silly grin and swagger he exhibited during my childhood, when he was up to something. He is tan, as usual, his muscular legs on display in a pair of gym shorts, and he looks fresh from a shower, his wavy hair still damp. His long drawn out, 'Hey,' is followed by, 'How's my little girl?'

I cannot move, or speak. I just stare at him as if he is a mirage. *He has to be a mirage.*

Claire walks in during my temporary paralysis. Amused, she looks at me, and then the grinning man. She isn't sure what to make of it, so she waits. Finally she asks, 'Here to try the focaccia?' He says, 'Hell yes, and whatever else you want me to try.'

Claire is smiling. She's lost somewhere between amazed and confused, clearly thinking, *Who is this character?* I say, 'Claire, this is my father, Ivan,' as she hands him a slice of focaccia. Claire tilts her head to the side, a smirk stretches across her face, 'Well, hello Ivan. Welcome.'

He takes a bite of focaccia and says, 'Thanks,' with his mouth full. Then, 'Uh, I better get going. I'm over at the campground, for now. Great focaccia. I'll be in touch.'

The bell rings as he exits. I stand dazed, staring at the door.

I am on my break.

Yes, it is clear to me other people are affected by the decisions I make, but in the end it is my life, the only one I'll ever have. I've made promises I cannot keep.

So I sit and wonder, *to what am I entitled?* Do I deserve this new life I've slipped into? Can I leave behind a life I feel is no longer mine?

THIS IS IT

The ad in the campground laundromat reads:

Would you like to live in a small, yet very charming, travel trailer? Room and board plus a little extra cash in exchange for the care of three horses, some gardening, and odd jobs around the property.

Call Shelly 233-5631

Dad calls. Shelly answers. He moves into the small, yet very charming, trailer, and is out feeding the horses that afternoon. Talking to himself, quietly, while looking out on the landscape he says, 'This is it.'

THEN I'M HAPPY TOO

Dad invites me over the next day. His trailer is at the back of the property, behind the five small cottages set up for weekenders. We sit in two weathered Adirondack chairs facing a series of bright green rolling hills. I love the color of winter in Northern California.

I don't ask how he found me, although I know he will tell me if I inquire.

Dad pops into his trailer and returns with two ice-cold bottles of dark beer. He hands me one. I think, *Sheesh, this man really settles in quickly.*

He looks into the hills and asks, 'Are you happier?' Focused on the hills I respond, 'Yes.' He pauses briefly and says, 'Then I'm happy too.'

We sip quietly until he looks toward me and says, 'Italian sausages on the grill?' I smile and nod, tears fill my eyes, and the hills blur.

JANUARY

The evenings grow colder. I listen to Billie Holiday.

MUSHROOMS

I wake up well-rested and hungry, sheet prints on my right cheek. I sit up in bed and look out the window. The sun is just beginning to filter through the fog. I decide to hike in the cold air while most of the town sleeps.

After a quick bowl of oatmeal with apples, olive oil, and salt, I take the high trail and wade through mist, fog, and thick green moss. The scent of wet forest leaves me craving mushrooms and I start outlining the steps necessary to bring forth a late lunch of white wine and mushroom risotto.

I've been told it is too late for porcini mushrooms, but the time is just about right for black trumpets and hedgehogs. I hope to find what I believe to be edible and stop by Astrid's for a more experienced identification. But I find nothing.

I stop by Astrid's anyway. She forages regularly and often sells what she finds to local restaurants or the market. I hope to catch her at home, with mushrooms. And I do.

She has golden chanterelles. 'You find them beneath the Coast Live Oak,' she tells me. 'But watch out for Poison Oak. Heavens! Don't touch those waxy leaves. You should join me next time. I'll show you how it's done.'

I insist on purchasing a handful. She refuses my money and sends me away with a small paper bag filled with much more than my request.

Once home, I gather everything I need:

Butter
Olive oil
Astrid's beautiful mushrooms
Fleur de sel
Black pepper
Yellow onion
Stock
Carnaroli rice
Parmigiano-Reggiano

I'm ready. I begin by brushing forest floor off the chanterelles and rough chopping them. I heat a sauté pan and warm butter and olive oil. Then add mushrooms, fleur de sel, and black pepper. I gently push it all around in the pan for about five minutes before leaving it to rest.

I melt more butter and oil in a heavy bottom pot. Chopped onions dance until just soft and translucent. Then the rice. Ladles of simmering stock are added one at a time as I slowly stir, each fully absorbed before adding the next. Then taste taste taste, until the rice reaches that perfect al dente state.

Right before the last ladle of stock I add the mushrooms. Stir. Final ladle of stock. Then the Parmigiano-Reggiano. One last gentle stir, and a brief rest beneath the lid, just a few minutes. Done.

I serve it with a drizzle of olive oil and a few grinds of black pepper. It is the best I've ever made. So good I know I'll be afraid to make it again.

WATCHING

The lagoon trail has the most beautiful palette, its colors shifting with season and time of day. Endless variations of blue, green, and gray, with occasional punches of bright yellow and magenta.

The sky is white and a cool mist fills the air. We are bundled up in hats and scarves. Near the trailhead a tiny cottontail rabbit pauses and locks eyes with me before darting off into the brush. A Great Blue Heron heading toward the lagoon glides above us.

The weather is calm at first, but shifts as we pass the lagoon and climb the dunes toward the ocean. The wind whips violently. The waves are wild and churning, crashing white and frothy against the shore. A bubbling cauldron. I sit on a large sea bleached drift log facing the ocean, Matt close beside me. We watch silently, captivated as the wind and waves perform. There are no lulls, full drama all the while. Gorgeous.

PREPARATION

I fill the bathtub and ease into the hot water, wincing a bit, and then settle. Clear hot water. The heat feels good, for a while, but soon I'm dizzy.

Lightheaded, I look at the trip lever with its long nose, round metal face, and two screwy eyes. The nose is crooked and the expression aloof. It looks at me, mockingly. I push the nose with my toe and let the water drain from the tub. Slowly, the heat evaporates from my skin and I begin to cool.

I stand up, mostly dry, and slip into panties, a white t-shirt, and make my way into the kitchen. I pour a tall glass of water and drink half of it in a single gulp.

Then I pick up my camera. The sun has just set. The light at this time of day is the most expressive. When shadows are low and long. And that last glimmer, at the moment closest to dark, it transforms what surrounds it like no other light.

SEED

Spring is just around the corner and I peruse seed catalogs, strategizing how I might arrange my garden in the spring, if I stay. Dad doesn't really understand my strategizing. He finds it unnecessary. He's always been happy counting on leftover seeds people happen to share with him, the occasional starts he finds at a nursery clearance sale, and whatever volunteers happen to pop up from last year's garden or compost.

Dad has always liked watching his plants go to seed. He enjoys knowing the seeds will scatter, lie dormant for a while, and then surprise him later. He rarely knows what is growing in his garden. He tosses new seeds into the soil, to compliment what is already there, but he usually forgets what he's tossed. Neat rows do not appeal to him.

When he finds a radish or young beetroot buried beneath a green top, he'll hose it down and eat it right then and there. He will clip whatever leaves look good, eat a few handfuls, throw the rest into a salad bowl, and dress it with olive oil and red wine vinegar. Dad believes eating weeds is perfectly acceptable. He decides what he likes by taste rather than familiarity or name. His salads have always been excellent. He hasn't become ill by eating the wrong plant. I don't know if he is indestructible or lucky, but whatever it is, I hope I've inherited it.

I don't like goodbyes. My favorite garden plants are cut-and-come-again, like a grass lawn, but edible. Plants such as lettuces and chicories. The process is incremental, less abrupt than going directly to seed. You cut a bit, and then a new bit grows in its place. It extends the relationship.

For most, a plant going to seed loses its appeal. Once the telltale signs of going to seed are evident in an edible plant, it often grows bitter. It becomes less desirable. There is also a sad drama in going to seed. The plant desperately transitions the majority of its energy to shooting straight up toward the sun, producing seed, and then spreading that seed before it dies.

STILL WINTER

7:30 a.m. Quiet. Still winter. A morning for hats and gloves.

Matt hands me his mug coated in royal blue enamel with white speckles. My favorite. It is filled with hot coffee and warm milk. He's holding his heavy ceramic lighthouse mug. His coffee is black.

As we walk outside, yellow-bellied birds dart past, near eye level. We spot an owl on the roof. He's clearly not fond of having his privacy invaded and spreads his wings wide to visit the better concealed perch of a nearby tree branch. We laugh and watch our breath in the cold air.

Meandering around the property, we keep our gloved hands wrapped around our mugs for extra warmth. There is frost on the grass and bright new buds on otherwise bare bushes. Early morning shadows stretch out around us.

I want to photograph all of it, but my hands are full. I promise myself I'll capture it on my next day off, that things won't change too much in a week, but I know it isn't true. I let my worry go and scan everything as I slowly turn a full circle, committing the moment to memory.

THE THIRTEENTH CHAPTER

I look up. The closest clouds race past at a frightening speed, yet the clouds in the distance remain completely still. I walk against a cold wind, the space between my shoulders contracted and pulled up toward my ears. A terrible feeling.

The cafe is cold and I stay wrapped in my scarf and jacket. *The Bell Jar* seems more painful this time around. I wonder how I managed to forget the extent of her dark unraveling. I am lost inside it for what seems hours when I finally shut the book on the thirteenth chapter, possibly for good, and head back out into the day.

The sun is high in the sky, bathing in its light all that was darkened earlier. The sharp wind has shifted to faint breeze. I stop and let the light seep into my bones and mind. It feels good, so good I want to lie down right in front of the cafe on what I imagine are very warm planks of wood and let all of Christine's customers weave their way around me.

NEXT DOOR

Dad and I cross the creek behind the lodge and head toward the meadow trail.

He asks, 'Do you like Shelly?'

'Sure,' I say.

'I like her too. She read her favorite Katharine Hepburn quote to me last night.'

"Sometimes I wonder if men and women really suit each other. Perhaps they should live next door and just visit now and then."

Then he asks, 'What do you think she meant by that?'

FINGER KNITTING

There was a reading in the barn last night. A Sri Lankan-born Canadian novelist and poet. The air was rough and cold. I wore my pale pink knit hat, a gift from Sam. She told me she wasn't thinking and knit it far to large for her granddaughter. It fits me perfectly.

Bales of hay were set up as bleachers, and a podium was centered below on a small wood stage. A large black piano rested beside the stage, a long neck lamp illuminating its keys.

We all listened to a beautiful set performed by a young melancholy musician from the city. During the break I met two little girls giggling and finger knitting. I believe they were related to the author, perhaps nieces. I'm not sure.

The author read from his latest novel. His words, emotion, and accent combined into a charismatic purr. It was all so lovely.

But on my way home I lost it all to my jealous thoughts. All I could think about was my desire to teach my girls to knit, and my fear they'd already learned without me.

DISTANCE

I rifle through new contact sheets, unsure what to print. The concise decision-making that won me this residency seems to have only been visiting. Temporary luck. It has gone.

My rifling could be attributed to not giving my work enough time to rest before critiquing it. Dom has a way around this. It is his way of insuring a later return to his work, with what he calls *fresh eyes*, and less of the emotional attachment that is inherent in work just made.

Although Dom makes photographs every single day, once he prints his contact sheets he files them away without review, and does not return to them for at least a year. He believes the time gives him needed distance from the work, and the ability to view his images more critically.

Dom has also told me he angles for allowing the whole book, museum, gallery craziness to enter his life only once per decade. Such social obligations, albeit necessary on some level, inhibit his work.

He is an artist, not a performer. It is the making he loves most.

I understand the premise of his process, but thinking in terms of decades scares me. Waiting for such large blocks of time. I cannot wrap my arms around it.

Dom doesn't entertain such fears. He works as if he will live forever.

WITHOUT

What was the movie? No, it was a book, Maugham's *The Moon and Sixpence*. Charles Strickland, the main character, left his wife and children. He knew they would be fine without him, and they were, better off in fact.

We are always told a larger support network makes us stronger, but is it true? Or are our often deeply buried survival skills only coaxed forward by uncomfortable or alienating situations? Are these situations the seeds from which our empowerment grows?

If I hadn't spent so much unsupervised time alone as a child and independently worked my way through those stressful young adult periods of fiddling with rules, contemplating normalcy, and making mistakes, where would I be today? If I'd been coddled and held secure, would I be a weaker person?

PALE GRAY AND BLUE

I cannot stop knitting. Small squares pile up in a basket beside my living room chair.

My hands move fast and furious when I know I have other issues to attend to. *Just one more row. One more*, I think. Then I knit another. Busy hands are excellent procrastination tools. They are deceptive because movement, movement of almost any sort, feels productive.

Today multicolored cotton coasters are taking the place of decision. I have two very important little lives waiting for me, yet I delay, row after row, watching the loops of pale gray and blue shift on and off my needles.

CHANGE

Will Dad stay in town if I decide to go? His relationship with Shelly is a mystery to me. I think it is a mystery to him too. He's changed with age. He doesn't mind her holding the reins. I think he prefers it.

They see each other when it suits her. An imbalance of power, perhaps, and a definite departure from his past relationships, yet I've never seen him happier.

INNOCENT AND BEAUTIFUL

I like spending time in the little glass house with Matt, but I also like being there alone. I might prefer it.

I often turn on his record player and place the needle upon whichever small revolving record he's left on the turntable. Knowing what he listened to last is like reading lines in his journal.

Today it is a young woman's voice. So earnest, innocent, and beautiful. I see it is a song from the decade in which I entered this world. I think of Mom, imagining what she might have been like the year I was born, and how it must have felt to become a mother at the age of eighteen.

I think of what the song means to him while setting the record to repeat, stretching out on the floor, reaching my arms far above my head, pointing my toes, and looking up at the ceiling.

REPLACEABLE

I've long doubted the removal of one person in a life could equate to an insurmountable dilemma. Most, if not all, are replaceable. My second grade best friend whose family moved to Tennessee, the boy with whom I shared my first kiss, the high school English teacher who championed my poetry—it was possible to move on and live a full life without these people. I am happy we spent time together. They helped me grow as a person, but it was learning to live without them that made me stronger.

WALKING TOWARD THE WATER

The first time I saw Matt he was walking across the beach toward the ocean, shortly after the sun had set, his eyes focused on the horizon line.

He wore a mustard colored cable stitched hat over dirty blonde windblown hair, a plain white t-shirt, and loose gray corduroy pants. As he drew closer I noticed his handsome scruffiness and looked away, not wanting my thoughts discovered. His canvas deck shoes were a weathered navy blue.

I turned back to see him standing at the water's edge, seemingly lost in thought. I lifted the viewfinder to my right eye, adjusted the exposure for the quickly shifting light, and pressed the shutter release.

CONTENTMENT

The wood in the fireplace burns slowly. We sit on opposite ends of the sofa, our feet touching in the middle, beneath a blanket. Every so often he looks up and smiles mischievously. I adore that smile.

Matt reads. I pretend to read while watching him. We take naps, eat popcorn, and wander around my garden to stretch our legs.

I don't want to go.

A LITTLE TEMPLE

I once heard someone speak of small bakery bread baking as a means of connecting community, the bakery serving as a little temple, providing local residents with a sacrament. And as I walk into Claire's bakery, sunlight shooting through clerestory windows, the illumination of suspended flour dust slowly settling, and the smell of warm wet yeast, I agree.

HINDSIGHT

It's unfortunate the way things make so much more sense once you step away from them. The deepest fissures do not form after a relationship has developed. They rarely wait. They are there in the beginning, very early.

But Joe and I had stepped away. We knew. How did we forget it all? How could two people possibly travel this path—twice?

WILD

I find a book of Northern California wildflowers on Matt's shelf and slowly sketch one with a fine point pen. I am pleased. Emboldened, I decide to sketch my glass of water. My drawing looks nothing like my glass of water. I suppose it is somewhat like my glass of water, if the glass were melted on one side and resting on a crooked shelf.

I've forgotten how to draw. I imagined it was a skill that would stick with me, that whole *like riding a bike* thing. It is not. Translating an object from a flat page of a book to a flat piece of paper is simple, but I have forgotten how to draw from life, how to apply perspective. I'll have to start over.

I think back, years earlier, to the final day of my *Introduction to Drawing* class, each student pinning their first and last drawings of the semester to the wall, proudly displaying the improvement made after months of practice. Our instructor thoughtfully commented on each set. She paused before my drawings. The first was very loose, almost feral, and the second more careful and well crafted. I sat tall awaiting her praise of the progress I had made. She did acknowledge my progress, but followed with, 'But I kind of miss Wild Sophia.'

PARENTS

My year away was not a promise to return to my life specifically as it was, but a promise to focus on myself, and be whole again, able to make proper decisions. As the year comes to a close I realize Joe will not be in my future, but they will, and he'll need to be in theirs. Eventually. Somehow.

He loves them. I love them. If we could live happily together we could share responsibilities, balance each other out, etc. But happily together is not our destiny.

How can it make sense to subject them to our dysfunction and allow them to grow and learn inside of it? I do not want them living in the strangeness of a childhood spent bouncing forward and back between us, weekly, or monthly, or whatever. There has to be another path.

There are so many ways to live a good life. Mustn't there be as many ways, if not more, of being a good parent? Is our culture too rigid in defining our parameters? I believe the answer is yes.

PEACE

I no longer feel the shoes I am wearing are a size and a half too small.

STILL ASLEEP

When I wake up the next morning my arm is draped over his still asleep body. The early sunlight filters through the trees, into the glass house, and perfectly illuminates his left forearm. I reach over and touch it, gently, smoothing the soft hairs in the direction they grow. I leave his warmth and tiptoe out into the cold air toward the sofa and find my camera. Kneeling ever so gently on the bed, my cold body contorted to find the same angle I saw his forearm when I woke, I quietly press the shutter release. He peacefully sleeps through it all.

WE SIT

We sit on a soft plaid wool blanket and look out at the ocean. The setting sun is warmer than it has been in months. Matt tucks my hair behind my right ear and looks at me, then out at the horizon as he begins to speak.

'The first time I saw you, you were sitting at the picnic table in the community garden. The sun was bouncing off all of the colors in your hair. Have you ever noticed how many shades of light brown and gold you have up there? Anyway, you looked so at peace, completely absorbed in the book you were reading, entertained, a sly smile on your face. I knew I wanted to crawl into that world with you.'

He knows.

APRIL

I walk outside, my small suitcase in hand, and shut the door of my cottage behind me. My throat is tight. I exhale a conflicted sigh, the gratification of completion woven into the sadness of finality. I do not turn for that necessary last look. I cannot.

EXPEDITED

My return to the valley feels expedited, nothing like my departure.

A NOTE

The apartment is available. I find our passports, pack lightly, and leave Joe a note:

I need to spend some time with them. We'll have to figure the rest out later.
We won't be gone long. Don't worry.
Thank you for understanding.

Sophia

THE LITTLE ISLAND

Without notice I arrive at the school and pick up the girls. I ask them simply, 'Would you like to visit Paris with me?' They both say, 'Yes.' No questions. They do not linger in uncertainty. They are decision makers, and so much better at it than I am. I admire them, but fear they are growing up too quickly, so quiet and poised for their young age.

We head directly to the airport, me with my small suitcase, and the girls with only the clothes on their backs.

We are as light as three tiny seed-bearing parachutes leaving their dandelions. And somehow we drift gently across the Atlantic. The journey seems strangely brief and we land before even settling into what is occurring.

A young man from the rental agency arrives by bicycle and walks us through a courtyard and into an apartment building. As we reach the base of the narrow stairway he takes my suitcase and we follow him up four flights of stairs, arriving before a cerulean door.

He unlocks the door and extends his hand for us to enter. The small familiar furnished apartment is awash with sunlight. It glows. The young man gives us a brief tour, hands me his business card and a large key, smiles, and he is gone.

We sit side by side on the sofa. I am in the middle. I look down at each of them and say, 'We should go out and explore the little island.' They look up, both excited and sleepy, and say, 'Yes Mama.'

I suggest we rest first, for just a few minutes. The girls nod, and we
slowly collapse onto one another, allowing the sunshine to lull us to
sleep.